Starving Writers
Literary Journal

Volume 4

"New Beginnings"

April 2019

Starving Writers Literary Journal- Volume 4

April 2019

A Truesource Publishing Book

Truesource Publishing : Dallas Texas

www.truesourcepublishing.com

ISBN : 978-1-932996-71-5

Printed in the United States of America
Published in Dallas, Texas

Editors
Marcus Blake
Jenn Chastka
Andrew Fallman

For More information on Starving Writers…

www.starvingwriters.net
www.facebook.com/starvingwritersjournal
www.twitter.com/starvingwritersjournal

"Write while the heat is in you. … The writer who postpones the recording of his thoughts uses an iron which has cooled to burn a hole with."

– Henry David Thoreau

Table of Contents

Check out more cartoons like this….
www.inkygirl.com

SHORT STORIES

The Littlest Snowman on Route 66

by

J. Franklin Green

THE MOVE

I was just eight years old when my parents moved from Ash Fork to Flagstaff. My father was a police officer in the Yavapai County Sheriffs' Department and my mother worked as a waitress at The Ranch Cafe in town while finishing her masters and doctorate degrees at

Northern Arizona University in Flagstaff. She had started this work well before

I was born and it took her a long time. Mom eventually got a job in the Chemistry Department at the University and my Dad left the police force to take a job as head of campus security. He didn't mind because it was safer than police work, my mom had finally achieved her goals and of course, he had me to think about too.

That was all fine and good for them but it wasn't fine and good with me. I had a lot of friends in town and loved the small town life. I especially liked all of mom's fellow waitresses and cooks at the Ranch Cafe. Fayrene Hume at the museum who was and is the town historian and "Saint Lucy" as everyone called her who had been just about everything in town in her time from a police posse member to postmaster were also important to me. Lucy was now retired and helped out just about anyone who needed darn near anything in town. My teachers were great as was our school and many of my classmates were fun, especially my best friend Marci. Now all of that was about to change because Flagstaff was a small city, not a small town and it was forty minutes away from Ash Fork on the freeway, Interstate 40. Now all of these details I am telling you now didn't enter the mind of my eight year old self, all I really knew was that Flagstaff was a long way from Ash Fork and I would never see my friends and everything else that was "home" to me.

I was crushed. My parents said we had to move and I would surely make new friends, even more because we were moving to a big suburban neighborhood with lots of houses and the elementary school was only a few blocks away. "Balony!" I said to myself at the time and cried the whole way there in the car.

Our house was a lot bigger than our old shabby house in Ash Fork but that didn't matter one wit to me. It was my house and I knew every nook and cranny including the weird animal images I saw in the knotty pine paneling and the imaginary secret portal in the back of my closet that led to a big old house with lace curtains, window seats and filled with toys. I could care less about freshly painted perfect walls, dishwashers and built in microwave ovens. The two car garage meant nothing along with the freshly paved neatly landscaped streets. I spent most of the month before school began arranging, rearranging and hating rearranging my room. My toys and books were all of the remaining comforting elements of home. Everything else was strange, foreign and a constant reminder that I was not home as I thought of home.

My parents were busy getting ready to start their new jobs. Dad was already away at the college campus most days setting up personnel changes and new procedures. Mom too was prepping for classes and sitting many faculty and administration meetings. All of this I did not know or care about at my age. I only knew that they were too busy to spend much time with me and on days that both were gone, I was alone except for

Mrs Caruthers who was my babysitter. Most of the time she just watched daytime TV game shows
or napped. So I arranged and rearranged some more and waited for school to start, with each passing day that it came nearer filling me with dread. I got a little tour of the school when my parents brought me in to register. It was enormous and brand spanking new, nothing like my old school. I was sure I would get lost and never be heard from again, but my dad tried to assure me that in a couple days I would be right at home there. "Baloney," I said again to myself. It would not and could not be like my school at my real home. I tried to convince myself they were right but I just couldn't. Why didn't they understand?

Finally, the big day arrived. I didn't get lost, well maybe once or twice, and my teacher was very nice and didn't once pull out a knife and fork and try to eat me for lunch or anything, but she wasn't Mrs. Morgan whom I knew well and was to be my new teacher back home in Ash Fork. Eventually I would get used to her and even come to like her but I sure didn't feel that way quickly. Recess was a nightmare. I had been introduced as new to the school to all the kids on the first day but most of them already had their group of friends and apparently didn't have any interest in adding anyone else. From overheard conversations, they weren't interested in the same things I was. Most of it seemed to center around things they had or cool things they were going to do, or cool things they were going to have. As bad as the ones who ignored me were, the ones who didn't were worse. A lot worse!

A "hick." Just a country bumpkin from a tiny little "hick" town who dressed funny and talked funny too. A lot of my clothes had come from the Family Dollar, The Virtual Closet second hand store, or were sewn by my mom or Mrs. Gunther our old next door neighbor. L.L. Bean, JC Penny and Sears were not where I got my clothes. I had a few outfits from a store down in Prescott but not many.

Second of all - I was just plain "the new kid" and they needed to push at me to see how far they could go so they could figure out how I would fit or hopefully not fit in with them. Most of them were upper middle class city kids and many of their parents, like mine, worked at the University. The fact that mine did also didn't count. I was still the "hick" with the weird name. In short order I became Windy, Wendy Bird, like in Peter Pan, or Goldie or Goldilocks even though my hair was dark brown.

My last name was Goldman, which of course which had led to the latter of the two names, but in addition to that, I was Jewish. The only Jewish kid in the class and as I later learned one of only five in the whole school. We weren't Orthodox, wearing black and yarmulkas and traditional dress or anything like that, and in thinking back on it, antisemitism really had nothing much to do with it. Eight and nine year olds don't really think in those terms except as they might have caught a hint of it at home. The point was that I was different in yet another way. Had I been a hick and a Hindu or Buddhist or believed in the Norse Gods like Odin and Thor it would have been all the same. I was the new kid, from a hick town who had a different religion. Three strikes before I even came to the plate. Had I been more mature, worldly wise or been more self-assured, I could have coped with it. But what eight year old is any of those things?"

So I suffered through fall and because as before, my parents were still absorbed in their new jobs and getting assimilated themselves, I suffered alone. As I think back, my mom might have been going through something similar to me because she too was a "hick" from a small town. My dad not so much. He was a cop after all and had dealt with a lot worse stuff in his life. Suffering may be a bit of a strong word but "alone" is a big word - a powerful and scary word. If you can't cure alone by finding friends you retreat further into "alone" until it almost feels comfortable. You hate it but you become used to it and it sinks in. Really deep!

WINTER ARRIVES

Winter in Flagstaff was very different. What snow we got in Ash Fork was dry and quickly blown away by high winds. The snow that came that first winter in Flagstaff was deep and wet. "We were at least 2,000 feet higher in elevation," my father told me. The boys called it "good packing" snow, ideal for snowballs and snowmen. Snowballs didn't excite me because I was sure I was going to be considered a moving target by most of the boys. The girls in the neighborhood mostly ignored me but some of the boys were mean. They teased, called me names, and delighted in shooting spitballs and rubber bands at me in school or on the way.

After a particularly big snowfall, as I watched the neighborhood boys building snowmen from our living room window, I decided so go outside and look at them. I have no idea what I was thinking at the time – not thinking was probably the answer, because as I was looking in wonder at the huge snowmen they were building, one boy, who always seemed to delight in tormenting me called out to his fellow, "Hey, look, Windy Wendee came out in the big bad snow." There followed a barrage of taunts, snowballs and laughter, so I retreated to the house and went to my room.

Still in my winter coat, I sat disconsolately and fuming on my bed looking about my room aimlessly, when I saw a Mr. Potato Head toy sitting in pieces on the floor of my closet. Even he seemed to mock me with a raised eyebrow and misplaced features. What I really wanted to do was smack the crap out of the neighborhood boys, but they were too big even for a tomboy hick from little old Ash Fork, but a weird and admittedly warped idea took form in my hurt mind.

Gathering up Mr. Mocking Potato head, I went through our kitchen, stopping at the utility drawer and went into the back yard where nobody would see me except maybe "Miss Kitty," the neighborhood cat, who seemed always to be pouncing on some sparrow or bluebird. Her I could handle, and in the mood I was in, she would not be a happy cat. Finding a nice open snowy spot I started to build a snowman. Just a little sucker, not some big thing like the boys out front were busy making. I wanted one only about a foot high for my purpose. My chest was heaving with anger and frustration as I started to build it, which didn't take overly long. When the snowballs were made and stacked, I used the Mr. Potato head eyes, nose (stupid moustache and all), ears and arms, sticking them in the wet heavy snow in place of the traditional buttons, carrots and sticks.

When that was done, I pulled out a plastic funnel from my pocket, the one purloined from the kitchen, turned it upside down and plopped in on its head. A Tupperware dunce cap it was, and it fit perfectly. That stupid little snowman just incontinently sat there in the middle of our small back yard with no idea of the fate I had in store for it. It had no idea, none, but I sure did. The whole time I was making it, tears were streaming down my face, dripping on my coat, scarf and the snowman. I had never heard of a voodoo doll, but in my mind this inanimate snowman represented all the boys (and girls by proxy) who seemed bent on making me miserable.

Clearing a path in the snow down to the brown sleeping grass as I went, I backed off about five feet and scuffed my boots to clear them of any sticky slippery snow. As I did this I looked up and saw "Miss Kitty" sitting on our fence watching me with that smarty pants cat look on her face and twitching her tail as though mocking me in her own hateful way. Snuffling back the ooze from my runny nose as I bent over, I made a small, compact and very hard snowball. My dad took be to a baseball game one time last summer, but I swear that no pitcher that day threw a ball harder, more accurate and fast that day than I threw at that cat. Of course, that is a bit of an exaggeration, but that snowball smacked that cat right in its face and knocked it clean off the fence.

"That's for the little bluebird you killed last summer you stinker," I yelled. Then I turned toward the little snowman, scuffed my feet again, and got ready to run forward and placekick him into smithereens. I could already see the funnel sailing toward the goal posts that were really a pair of barren saplings, and Mr. Potato Head features flying in all directions like pieces of a piñata at a birthday party.

Leaning over and clenching my fists preparatory to starting my run, I saw the moustache twitch and the Mr. Potato head eyes, pop off and land in the snow in front of the snowman. In their place, two eyes opened, clear, large and bright blue, sparkling in the sun. Stunned and curious, I walked forward slowly, all thought of field goals and kick offs evaporated.

"I like the moustache," it said. "Can I keep it?"

I was speechless.

"I'm not sure about the hat though. Something with a wider brim would keep the hot sun off of my head."

The first thought that came to me was maybe I had fallen asleep in my room and was just dreaming this, but my nearly frozen toes argued against that hypothesis. My mouth went dry and my palms began to sweat. "What... where did you... who are..." I stammered.

"Let's start with 'who' if you don't mind," it said. "You can call me 'Frosty, Snow-Boy, Billy-Bob, Jimmy John' or whatever you please, but not 'Bogus.' That name, is already taken. Maybe you saw the movie with the big goofy Frenchman and Haley Joel Osment?" A smile popped out beneath the Mr. Potato Head nose and moustache. "Personally, I rather fancy 'Bernard' – a nice name don't you think?"

"Bernard?" I said, still rather confused and not a little

mystified.

"Bernard W. Allman, if you wish to be formal, but not Bernie please." He winked as he said this and I sat down hard in the snow.

"Now as to your other queries, where I came from I have no clue really but the why is very simple. Your tears brought me. You are hurt, lonely and need a friend – so… here I am! But if you want me to stick around for a while, you better get me a broader brimmed hat and get me out of the sun. Maybe it would be better under the eaves next to your dad's shed? The sun never hits that spot."

My eight year old brain was befuddled, scared and massively confused, so I turned and ran into the house and upstairs to my room. I sat on my bed for a moment shaking. As I did I saw an old doll of mine with a big straw hat on its head, sitting on a shelf. "What are you waiting for," it seemed to say. There was no wink, no moving lips, and no nod of the head. If there had been I might have gone screaming to my mother and this story never written, but instead, I pulled the hat off and brought it outside. Replacing the funnel on Bernard, the snowman's head with the hat, I then picked it up, or him rather, and carried him carefully to the shade under the eaves. "Thank you, he said, "Much better here "

Now what?' I asked.

"First we have to get to know one another. All I know is that you are hurting inside but that's about it. Please tell me why."

An hour later, near dusk, I had finally told him everything about myself, from my home and friends in Ash Fork to this horrible life in Flagstaff. Just getting it out in words lifted a great weight. Until then I had kept it all bottled up inside except a few times I tried to talk to my mother and father about it. They had been kind, but told me that "these feeling would pass in time," and "I would see it differently later, blah, blah, blah…" they didn't understand how I felt from my point of view which was now, not in some distant, non- existent future. Kids are not very good at the whole "put it in perspective" thing. They only understand and feel how they feel and think that day, or that minute. It's just like when I had my first crush on Jimmy Sanders and he moved out of town with his folks. I was devastated, but all they could say, that it "wasn't important now because blah, blah, blah, I would get over it soon, blah, blah and more blah." I was sad then and it was big to me then.

Bernard said none of those things. He just listened and asked questions from time to time between my sobs.

Before I knew it, I heard my dad's car pull up, my mom was already home, and knew I would be called in for supper soon. I looked toward the back door and started to say…

"Yes, supper time. Just a thought or two for you to chew on while you're chewing and that pepperoni pizza your dad brought home with him."

"What other people think about us is none of our business. What we think of ourselves is what counts. Hang on to the good and toss out the rest. Just sitting in your own lonely poop and being angry might seem comfortable because it is, after all, your own poop, but it still stinks. Reach out to find friends. If they don't respond, try again or move on. Until they do, you have me, and I think you are a bright, pretty, sensitive and thoughtful girl, just like Fayrene, Lucy, your teachers and friends in Ash Fork did. Hold on to that if you need to until you find your own self. Now get on to super before it gets cold. I like cold pizza, but I bet you don't!"

As we ate supper, my daddy was watching the news. When it was over the weather forecast came on – cold and cloudy for the next week with the possibility of more snow. Mom and dad weren't happy about that – but I was!

A NEW BEGINNING

Every day after school I spent my afternoons with Bernard. On Wednesday, I told him I looked at the fourth grade class list to find out if there were any other Jewish kids on it. There were two. Irene Reiff and Maya Rodich. I found both of them on the playground at recess and invited them to Friday night Shabbat at my house. I had asked my mom's permission, of course. Maya politely declined, but Irene said that even though her family wasn't all that religious, she would ask her dad. All Bernard said about it was, "Good start kiddo."

Friday night came and Irene and her dad drove over. My dad invited her dad to stay also if he wished, but he had to go to a basketball game – his son Brandon was on the eighth grade team. Afterward, I brought Irene out to meet Bernard, but as I figured, he said nothing. She did however compliment his hat and moustache. As we were going back into the house, I glanced back at him and he winked at me. That was the beginning. Many of the other frustrations, teasing and ostracizing from the "in cliques" continued and they hurt my feelings – but not as much. Not nearly as much. I had at least one friend and of course, I had Bernard.

The following Friday, Irene's whole family joined us. My family was not very religious either, but my Mom and Dad maintained some Jewish traditions, especially for keeping the family close. Eventually my dad, and Irene's father, Marc became friends too, but all I saw that night was Brandon. He was four years older than me, but a crush is a crush is a crush. He was tall and gangly but had this huge smile and most importantly didn't talk to me like I was some hick from Ash Fork. He even asked some questions about my hometown, which I was more than glad to elaborate on.

My crush on him lasted until I got Mr. Finnegan in the fifth grade.

The only disturbing thing that night was the weather report. A warming trend was the forecast with highs in the low 60's in the day and 40's at night. All I could think about was Bernard. All my mom could think about, was why all the ice cube trays in the freezer were frequently not frozen. I emptied them as fast as they froze, and put scrap plywood and anything else I could find around Bernard and dumped the ice cubes around him as fast as they were ready. I saw with dismay however, that he was getting smaller every day. He kept talking to me right up to the end and assured me he would be back whenever I needed him and it was cold and snowy enough. I raced home from school Wednesday after the bell rang, but Bernard was gone. Only his hat and the Mr. Potato Head nose, moustache and ears were there, sitting in a puddle of water. That puddle got a little bigger, as my little girl tears flowed and flowed with the anguish of losing my best friend, the one who had changed my life and started it off in a better direction. Arizona was in a long drought at that time, and the rest of the winter was mild with no snow. Dad said the ski resorts like the Arizona Snow Bowl were really hurting, but I am here to tell you they weren't hurting like I was.

BACK TO BACK

I thought about Bernard almost every day but I remembered his advice and comfort always. Through the spring and summer, I made a few more friends and joined two clubs. The Junior Scientists Club at school and an Okinawan Karate club at a Dojo near the University. One fueled my head, and one fueled my confidence and kept me trim. I also offset my penchant for Hershey bars and Doritos. Slowly the thought of Bernard faded and I only thought of him when I had a crisis, loss or run in with the school bullies. I thought the bullies would leave me alone as I advanced in my training and earned higher level belts, but for some of them it was like waving a red flag in front of a bull. Some moron was always wanting to see how tough I really was. I talked most of them down or just refused to fight unless I had to. That is what my training said to do and most of the time it worked.

Summer ended abruptly with the coming of 5th grade and Mr. Finnegan. My crush was deep, but what kept it going was the fact he was also the advisor for The Junior Scientists Club. Or maybe that was why it started! Who knows? It faded in time but my interest in science didn't as you can guess from the preface to this story. Things were in general going very well and I rarely missed Bernard. But as the saying goes, all things come to and end and the only certainty in life is change. The two things happened back to back.

Billy Moran was in the Science Club, but mostly only because his dad was in the science department at the University. He had been pressured into it but he wasn't really into it. What he *was* into was being a bully and throwing his considerable weight around. Apparently, Ho Ho's, Ding Dongs and Hostess cakes were his best friends. One afternoon he was being his usual obnoxious self, so most of us ignored him, but the more we ignored him the angrier he got. When my pal Tanner got in his way while he was cleaning up the lab, Billy gave him a shove and he stumbled over into me. Tanner was short, skinny and wore Coke bottle bottom glasses. An easy target for a guy like Billy. I got a little annoyed and said, "Knock it off Billy, do you feel good picking on someone half your size?"

"How about you little Miss Karate?" he shot back.

Here we go again, I thought to myself, only said, "Forget it Billy, I don't want any trouble." And neither do you fat creep, I thought to myself. As though he was reading my mind, Billy came right up on my and without warning smacked me in the face with his open palm. In Karate, this is often the prelude to an attack, so my training stepped up and I gave him a kick push to the chest to get him away from me. Now a kick push is just that – a push, but using your feet. Billy started to bluster and threaten, but neither of us had seen Mr. Finnegan enter the room. He saw the entire exchange and was obliged to haul us both down to the Vice Principal's office. The long and the short of it was that Billy got a lecture and I got SUSPENDED for a week. Why, was all I could ask myself, Billy was the aggressor and I was just defending myself.

My dad wanted to know why too and went to the school to inquire. As an ex cop it made no sense to him either. As it was explained to him, the issue was the use of the feet. The rules were specific and inflexible (no doubt written by some desk jockey my dad said later). Kicking was kicking and carried a mandatory one week suspension. Slapping and threatening was apparently okay. The only saving and ironic grace to the absurd affair was that a blizzard hit Northern Arizona that night and all schools were closed for four days –most of my suspension.

I was still upset and fuming about this when I thought of Bernard. The first time I had thought of him in a long time. So I gathered up the Mr. Potato head things, his straw hat and headed out back right after breakfast the following morning. As quickly as I could I built a snowman, the littlest snowman ever built on Route 66 I reckoned. Attaching the eyes, nose, ears and arms, I was plopping the straw hat on his head and waited. Nothing happened. Bernard had promised to come back. He promised. Deeply disappointed, I sat in the snow and tears welled up in my eyes.

"Omber a bif" I heard. "Omber ambnt telb inchs." What the heck? I thought. Then I understood and moved the snowman twelve inches to my left to exactly where he was last year.

"That's better," he said as the Potato Head eyes popped out and fell revealing his crystal blue eyes. "I forgot to tell you that I would always be back for you but only if you built me in the same place. Your tears are part of the ground where I sit. They always will be."

Now I really cried. I cried with relief and joy. Bernard and I sat for hours until I was nearly frozen and he suggested I get myself back in the house. When I told him of the events of the past year he laughed and told me I was the quickest learner he even encountered. About the suspension, he said little except to tell me that there are always things in life that seem or *are* unfair that was just how life is, if you're not a little snowman. "Build a bridge and get over it," he said, and "Move on."

The winter was a long and cold one and Bernard stayed around until early March. I had many friends by this time, but I vowed to never forget Bernard again, and I almost never did again until…

ALWAYS AND AGAIN

Every winter after that, I built Bernard in the same spot whenever the snow came. He was with me through Junior High and right up to High School Graduation and beyond. Whenever I had a problem, a question or a joy to share I shared it with him. Boyfriends, career choices, losses of loved ones, achievements, disappointments or just plain catching up each year, I shared it all with Bernard. When I left for college, I made a point of returning in the winter at least once. That almost ended when in the summer between my junior and senior year, my father retired and my mom took a job at Arizona

State University in Mesa, Arizona in the biochemistry department. I visited then that winter but took off for a day "to visit and old friend in Flagstaff" I told them.

I watched the weather reports and knew they had snow.

Sneaking into the back yard, I spoke with Bernard for what I feared was the last time, but he told me soon I wouldn't need him anymore. I asked him why but he wouldn't tell me, he just winked that knowing wink of his.

I got busy at graduate school and didn't get a chance to get back home for several years, but one winter after I had just broken up with my fiancée, I flew back and drove north to Flagstaff and there I was crushed! The new owner of my parent's house had expanded the kitchen back and the new room covered over where Bernard had to be built. When I came around front to get in my rental car, the owner pulled up. He looked vaguely familiar but it was hard to see him clearly through my tears.

When he saw my flooded eyes, and red running nose, he asked, "Can I help you?"

"Not unless you have a jackhammer," I replied through my sniffles."

"Now you have my curiosity piqued. Is there a story behind the need for a jackhammer?"

"It's silly, unbelievable and a real long story," I said to him. "You would never believe it anyway."

"Why don't you try me," he said. I'm a professor of literature at the University and a writer when I have time. It might make a good story. Come in please, I'll make some coffee and I have some Krispy Kreme doughnuts in this bag."

Why I trusted him or took him up on his offer I don't know. Maybe it was the oddly familiar face, or the fact that I had travelled a long way to talk to Bernard and needed to vent. Whatever the reason, we sat in his living room for three hours as I told him the whole story and the reason for my tears. He never once doubted me and only a couple of times asked a question or two to clarify what I was saying. This surprised me not a little.

"I've been here for three hours, ate four doughnuts and downed three cups of coffee," I said. "But I don't even know your name."

He smiled winningly and said, "My name is James Sanders, but you used to call me Jimmy when we were little. I had a little crush on you back then and I thought you had one for me too, but we were only eight years old when you moved away. I never knew where or why until today."

We had a light supper in Old Town that evening, but as I got in my car to drive to the small motel room I was staying in, he leaned on the door and said, "I know you are driving back to Mesa tomorrow, but if you don't mind would you stop by on your way. Please?" I told him I would stop by around eleven, and he said that would be fine.

I pulled into his driveway and James was waiting for me on the front porch. I got out and as I approached, he said nothing until I got to the steps.

"Please, come in. I never showed you the new dining room I added to your parent's house. I think you might like it."

I wasn't sure if I really wanted to see the addition, especially because of what it covered. "He should know that," I thought. But he seemed so nice and sincere about it I decided to humor him. When he opened the new French Doors, I found it hard to breathe for a moment. The room was empty of furniture, all the windows were wide open and there was a pile of snow in one corner. There was a big hole in the concrete floor and a jackhammer leaned in the other corner.

He stepped back and said, "I'm pretty sure Mr. Potato Head and a straw hat is in that oversize bag you're carrying. Take your time. I'll have coffee brewing in the kitchen when you're done."

Burgermen

By

Alan Zacher

It's 5:42 a.m., and the police have finally left. I know it's actually Monday, but it still feels like its Sunday. I'm sitting at my long old wooden desk, looking out of the tall, narrow window that faces east, in my bedroom on the second floor of my parents' big old house.

God, I'm drained — physically, mentally and spiritually. What a night it was — the screaming sirens, the throngs of police, the chaos, the confusion, the anxiety, the questions, the blood, the body. I don't think this old neighborhood has ever experienced anything like this ever happening before, or, at least, I can't remember one ever happening before like this one — and I've lived here all of my life, 53 years. This is a quiet old neighborhood, with quiet old people. Crimes like this one simply don't happen here. I mean, this is Lemay, an old suburb of St. Louis County: Lemay is adjacent to the beginning of the City of St. Louis. The line of demarcation being the Des Peres River, which snakes its way east to the Mississippi River, just a few miles north of here.

Many of our neighbors were milled on the old cracking sidewalk in front of our house tonight — some dressed in hurriedly-put-on street clothes, or robes over pajamas and slippers; all huddled together sharing sleepy-eyed-ness, and tempered speculations, and a dying curiosity to know. Mrs. Peterson, who is a widower,--the nosy, old biddy- buddy — and who lives to the left of our house, was there; and Mr. and Mrs. Meyers were there, who live two houses to the left of Mrs. Peterson, and on and on. And, boy, you should have seen the look of pure shock on the faces of all of those old people when the ambulance people carted that dead body out of here.

It was touch-and-go there for a while, but I was sure relieved, and glad, when the police didn't arrest Dad or take him away for killing Fred. They did take his bayonet, though, which really upset him: My father had brought that bayonet home with him from the Army, World War II — my dad had even fought in The Battle of the Bulge…God, it's hard to believe that that now shriveled-up old man whose afraid of the dark actually fought in the Bulge, and had killed people.

They, the police, had wanted to know why he was carrying that bayonet to begin with, and why does he keep saying: "I killed a burgerman." I told them—well, we both told them,--Mom and I—that he has Alzheimer's and that he's scared at night—has fears that the boogieman is going to get us—and straps on his old Army belt with its sheaf and bayonet at night over his pajamas and robe and checks to make sure that all of the doors and windows throughout the house are closed and locked: When Dad had first started strapping on his old Army belt with that sheaf and bayonet at night, Mom and I, from shear fear, had tried to dissuade him from doing that, but it upset him so much, and the wearing of it seemed to have such a calming effect on him, that we gave up and let him continue doing it—and anyway, he never drew the bayonet.

They, the police, asked a whole lot of other questions, too, that were very difficult for me to answer:

Police: You say that you were upstairs in your bedroom, sleeping, when you were suddenly awakened by a noise coming from downstairs. You came downstairs to checkout the noise. You stepped into the kitchen and heard a noise from behind, in the hallway. When you turned around, you were immediately confronted, and assaulted, by the victim, who you say, was holding a gun. Is this right?

Me: Yes, it is.

Police: But there aren't any signs of a forced entry. And a search of the victim's person has revealed a key that you have confirmed is a key to the front door. How do you account for that?

Me: Because of my father's Alzheimer's, rarely do we ever leave him here alone in the house. But last Saturday, I had a dentist appointment at 9 a.m. and my Mom had a prayer meeting at the same time at St. Andrew's Church, so we had to leave him alone — he usually sleeps during the day anyway. When I got home that day, he told me that the guy was here checking the locks on the doors. When I asked him: "What guy?" he didn't know. He just kept saying: "You know. The guy who checks the doors." I thought he had just dreamt it. I had asked Mrs. Peterson next door if she had seen some guy at our house that morning, but she has colon cancer and had diarrhea and was "on the pot" most of the morning. But with what has happened now, I think it was him, Fred. He must have taken the key to the front door from Dad.

Police: You say that you know the victim, but, then again, you don't know him. What exactly does that mean?

Me: He was the manager of Discount Foods, the one on Navaho Street, right across the river, in the city. I say "was" the manager because he walked off the job two weeks ago Friday after an elderly man, a customer, complained to him that he couldn't retrieve his quarter from the cart dispenser and he, Fred, ripped the coin disperser from the handle of the cart and shoved it up one of the nostrils of the elderly man to the point of where even the quarter couldn't be seen anymore. This was all told to me by a young girl employee who works there and who I happened to meet one day by chance, about eight days ago. I worked there for a week three weeks ago. I was a stocker/cashier. But doing the freight was just too hard on my back. That's how, and all, that I know of the man. I didn't even know what his last name was until you told me.

Police: You say that you believe he was here tonight to rob you. What makes you say that?

Me: One day, while at work on a lunch break, in the small room in the back of the store that serves as a lunchroom, I had told some of the employees, who were also on a lunch break, how my parents are old, and about my Dad having Alzheimer's, and about how I was getting all of their finances in order — how what a difficult task this is; that just in the house alone my Dad has a coin collection that is worth, probably, 40 thousands dollars, and how my mother has lots of jewelry, diamonds and such. Fred was also in that room when I had said all of this, and that probably gave him the idea to rob us.

I don't believe they totally believed me, but at least they said Fred's killing appears to have been justifiable homicide, and they didn't take Dad away or anything.

It's all such a mess. Because, yes, much of what I told them was indeed lies — which reminds me, I have got to get rid of Fred's cell phone: I didn't want the police having it. But how could I have told them the truth? How could I have told them that for the past two weeks that guy had made my life — our life, here at home — a living hell? How could I tell them that he had been terrorizing me — us — for the last two weeks because I quit that lousy job? Yeah. That's right. The reason that that jerk was terrorizing me and threatening to kill me was because I had quit that job. The guy was nuts.

You should have heard how ballistic he got when I called him and told him that I wasn't coming in anymore because doing that freight was just too hard on my back—two weeks ago, Friday, it was. He said: "You haven't even worked here a week and you're quittin'?!"

"I'm very sorry," I replied. "It's just too hard on my back."

"So you're not comin' in? You're leavin' me short-handed?"

"I'm very sorry," I repeated. "It's just too hard on my back."

"Ok," he said. "Here's the deal, see. I'm givin' you one chance—and one chance only—to make good. It's 5:40. You're scheduled to be in here at 6. You got 20 minutes to get in here, see. Are you goin' to be a man and do the right thing or not? Are you comin' in?"

"I'm very sorry," I repeated. "It's just too hard on my back."

"Fine," he said. "Let it be on your head. See, you're a spineless, weak, wishy-washy punk. You're all the same—just like that spineless, wishy-washy, no-good, bitch wife of mine. That bitch ran off with my kids last night. When I find her—and I will find her—I'm gonna kill her—just like I'm gonna kill you. Watch your back, punk." Click.

I got to tell you, I was shocked. Shocked!—and scared. I'll admit it, the guy scared me. I don't know why he scared me, but from the moment I met him, he scared me. He wasn't all that big of a guy, or tough-looking. In fact, he was rather on the lean side and had a boyish-looking face, with blue eyes and red hair. Plus, although that crappy, non-union store is in a quickly deteriorating part of the city, I don't believe he, Fred, grew-up around there, or even in the city for that matter. He didn't strike me as someone having street-smarts or street-toughness: Although his no-good, expletive, expletive, old man had abandoned him and his mother when he was 12, his mother idolized him, he had told me. His mother worshiped the ground he walk on, and listened and did everything he told her to do: She's an angel, and angel — in heaven, he had said of her. So, no, it wasn't his physical size or toughness that scared me so, but his demeanor, his personality, his soul. Everything about the guy shouted, demanded, control. A demeanor that was as fiery as his red hair. A demeanor of narrow-mindedness that enjoyed — no, reveled in controlling and bullying others. A demeanor that was a stick of dynamite, with the match already lit and only an inch away from the wick.

No, I'll admit it. He scared me, and he was only 30-something. I'm 53-years-old, and he scared me. And what was with him calling me a punk? What was that all about?

God, what a mess it all is.

I only took that damn job because I couldn't think of how to lie my way out of it: The guy who owns that store owns three others and the person who was the district manager of the four stores is a short, pudgy, 50-ish woman named Ruth who is also a member of one of the many prayer groups that my mother belongs to; and when my mother happened to mention to Ruth that I desperately needed a part-time job—for extra money when I began student teaching in the fall—Ruth told Mom that she could get me a job at one of the stores.

So, I couldn't help but take it. But, boy-oh-boy, taking it sure messed up my plans of finding a full-time job and moving out of the house and being on my own—so that I wouldn't feel obligated to Mom to student teach this coming fall and obtain my teaching certification, Secondary, English. I know all of this sounds convoluted, complicated and messy; and that's because it is convoluted, complicated and messy.

My whole life has always been like that—convoluted, complicated and messy…Well, I guess it's really not complicated. Actually, it's quite simple: I've never known who I am. I've never known what I wanted; and I've always been a coward. My whole life has been about running and telling lies—running from jobs, people, life and myself, and then telling lies to cover-up the running.

What a mess.

I mean, I'm 53-years old; I still live at home with my parents; I don't have a job; I don't have a girlfriend, or a friend at all; I don't have any money; and I don't have any prospects of ever attaining any of those things.

I've always been ashamed of my life, and I live in constant fear of "the other shoe falling," as the saying goes—of my life and running and lies being exposed, revealed.

I've always been like this. It's horrible. It's the story of that old platitude of a coward dying a thousand deaths—well, I haven't died a thousand times, but I bet I've had close to a thousand jobs in my life. Well, at least, a hundred jobs, and I quit every damn one of them. Sometimes I'd work a couple of months; sometimes a couple of weeks; sometimes only a day; sometimes I wouldn't even show up at all. It was the same with women. I've never been very good at "putting-the-make" on girls, as the saying goes. The girls that I was interested in and got to consent to go out with me,--which were few—once they got too close, I always ran like a jack-rabbit—the very thought of being in a committed relationship would cause me to freeze more solid than a jack-rabbit trapped in the hypnotic-freeze of a car's headlights.

More and more, of late,--something that I've never told anyone about—I'm beginning to believe I am the way that I am not so much because of my parents and older sisters, Mary and Eve, having babied me so much, which they did, but because of my brother, James, being run-over and killed by a hit-and-run driver when I was 10-years-old. James was two years older than me, and what has plagued me so much about his death, to this very day, was him being trapped in that closed casket. At his internment, when I asked Mom how long he had to stay in that box, she replied: "Until the end of time." Without having the ability to verbalize it, or rationalize it, I think that I told myself that that would never happen to me—being trapped, that is.

So, run, run, run; and lie, lie, lie. That's my life. The only thing, I fear that I'm running out of places to run, and I'm getting damn tired of lying, too. But I have always had hope — hope of finding THE job; hope of finding THE girl; hope of finding THE life; hope of finding — of finding — me.

I guess about the only thing in my life that I can be proud of is all of my education — my degree in English, from when I had wanted to be a high school teacher the first time, and all of my associate degrees and certifications and such — in business and computers and philosophy, and on and on; and I've never done a damn thing with any of them.

If only I had completed my teaching certification the first time, back in 1976, I wouldn't be going through the mess that I'm presently in — and it was far easier to obtain certification back then than it is now. Back then, one only had to get a degree, a B.A., and student teach to obtain certification; and, back then, one only had to student teach for 6 weeks. Now, besides there being far more courses to take than there was back then, one not only has to student teach for an entire semester, one has to submit a portfolio,--written documentation after documentation of what you have done to qualify to teach — and it's 30 percent of one's final grade. God, when I think about it, I could just kick myself for not completing my certification back then, in 1976. I had completed all of the courses, and all I had to do was student teach. I began student teaching, but I only lasted two days. I hated it. I hated everything about it. I withdrew from the teaching program, telling the school, St. Louis University, that my father had had a heart attack and I was needed at home. I told Mom, and everyone else, that the school felt that I wasn't skilled at teaching

English, and that I should perhaps select another field to teach, such as History, which I told everyone I had no interest in teaching.

Run, run, run; and lie, lie, lie. It's been my whole life.

I guess I can thank my lucky stars that my parents are now old and mentally challenged, because if it weren't for that, and them never having been too bright of people,--lower-middle-class, blue collar workers: My dad dug ditches at the Gas Company for 35 years, and my mother was a checker in a grocery store for 20 years — I'd be living on the streets.

My torpid life use to really bother me, but not so much anymore. I guess I've just gotten use to being a loser in life. Mental depression has plagued me most of my adult life. Sometimes it would get pretty bad, intense — going out into the back yard and pounding my fists against the big old maple tree out there until my knuckles bleed; going nightclubbing downtown and getting stinking drunk, and on and on. I dealt, mostly, with my goofy life, and mental depression, with alcohol, getting stinking drunk night after night, whiskey mostly. But I don't drink much whiskey anymore, just beer, mostly.

Only twice in my life did my mental depression get the better of me to the point where I had to seek professional help, a psychiatrist.

The first time was when I had turned 40. When I had turned 40, I went through a period in my life when I thought that I was dying — I mean, I thought I had everything from having a heart attack to cirrhosis of the liver to cancer to kidney failure to AIDS. You name the disease, and I thought I had it. Poor Dad. What a good guy he was about it all. I bet he drove me to the emergency room, sometimes at 2 a.m., — a million — well, not a million times, but a lot. The last time that he did, the doctor — a young, arrogant guy, who had seen me two or three times before — said to Dad: "Sir, he's not physically ill. He needs psychiatric care." Dad didn't understand what he was talking about until the guy said: "There's nothing wrong with him. It's all in his head."

So, Mom and Dad made me start seeing this psychiatrist that our family physician gave them the name of. But that guy didn't help me at all. Outside of prescribing pills that doped me up greatly, he did nothing but ask me questions about my childhood, my dreams, my feelings about life, and my sexuality. I went to him for about 4 months. Then, I just stopped going. Whatever it was that first made me believe that I was dying, simply stopped. Then, when I turned 50, three years ago, I got tired, or scared, of my excessive abuse of alcohol — fear of what it was doing, or had done, to my mind and body. Plus, I was just damn fed-up with my empty life. I mean, even 5 or 4 years prior to that time, I was at least still making half-assed attempts at trying to find a job, a girl, a life. But then, I settled into this life of sleeping late, watching TV, reading the newspaper after supper, watching more TV, getting pie-eyed drunk and falling to sleep in a drunken stupor. This I did night after night.

I chose my own psychiatrist this time. I chose him because the Yellow Pages listed his office as being only a mile away from my parents' house. He, Dr Wi, was a tall, lean, middle-aged, balding man of Asian descent, who seemed to be more American than I, and who charged $80.00 an hour: Poor Dad. Whenever I'd ask him to write me a check for Dr. Wi, he'd always say: "I sure hope that that Chinaman is helpin' you, Tom. Damn. Eighty dollars an hour, just to talk...."

Looking back upon it, I guess he did help me, somewhat. It was because of Dr. Wi that I, basically, stopped drinking whiskey, and why I went back to school. But at the time, I thought he was, for the most part, full of hot air.

"Jesus H. Christ, man," he said. "Yes, you're an alcoholic. Go to AAA — I know that you won't, but you need to stop drinking, completely. You won't do that either, but try and stop...Jesus H. Christ. You're like you are because you have a chemical imbalance, and because, sure, you were babied too much...Jesus H. Christ, man. Sure you'd still like to have a career, a woman, a life. But you don't get it, do you? You don't try anymore because the boat has sailed. You're set in your ways now. You're retired. I wish my old lady, my wife, would let me retire...Jesus H. Christ. Go back to school?! Be a teacher?! What's most important to you now is to be free. You're only setting yourself up for a lot of unnecessary disappointment and failure. If you do go back, you won't finish. Be satisfied with who and what you are and what you have. You got a great life, man. You got the life you wanted — to be free. Although you said that your father had recently been diagnosed with having Alzheimer's, the best scenario for you is to keep your parents healthy and alive as long as possible. Hopefully, they, or one of them, will live until you're of age to collect Social Security. That way, you'll…."

See what I mean about that guy being goofy. How could I be retired? I think you have to have a job first before you can retire. And anyway, I don't want my life to be like that—never having done anything with it. No, he was goofy.

Well, shortly after him telling me that I was retired, I stopped seeing him, just stopped going, which he told me that I'd someday do. Anyway, I was bound-and-determined to prove him wrong about me. I enrolled in the teaching program at the University of Missouri-St. Louis and began taking classes. It took me three years to complete all of the courses to obtain certification, Secondary, English, but I did it. I had another 30 credit hours of college under my belt. All I had to do now was turn in my portfolio and do my student teaching, which would be another 12 credit hours. I turned in my portfolio and began student teaching this past January at Truman High, in the city. I was so proud of myself.

Well, I did much better this time at student teaching than I had the last time so many years ago—at least this time, I lasted three weeks before I quit.

Nothing bad happened there to make me want to quit. I just wanted to. I hated it. I hated getting up every morning at 5 a.m. to be there by 7 a.m. I hated putting in 8 hours a day for no pay. I hated having to take orders from my co-operating teacher, Mrs. Brown: an elderly black woman,--Elderly? She's only four years older than me.—who has taught at Truman for 22 years and is a

skilled teacher and who was good to me. But I just hated
it. I shook the whole time I was there. I didn't eat; I
couldn't sleep; couldn't concentrate. I hated it.

So, there I went again. Run, run, run; lie, lie and lie.
That's my life.

I told Mrs. Brown and the college that my father's
Alzheimer's had suddenly worsened, and because of that,
and because of being much needed at home, I felt it best
to withdraw from school and begin again in the near
future — perhaps next semester, or so. They were all very
sympathetic and understood, especially Mrs. Brown.
Family comes first, she had said.

Very sad, angry and upset, I had told Mom that the
reason I was late getting home that day was that Dr.
Burke, who is the dean of the Education Dept. at the
college, had called me at Truman and wanted to see me at
the college after school to talk with me about the initial
evaluation of my portfolio. When I got to the college, Dr.
Burke told me that the evaluation of my portfolio
revealed that I had insufficient comprehension of the
methodologies, concepts, and applications of teaching.
This being the case, if I submitted my portfolio in its
present form for grade, I would more than likely receive a
D. Since the portfolio is 30 percent of one's final grade,
this would mean that I would have to ace all four of the
teaching evaluations I would receive by the college
during student teaching in order for all of it to average
out to a final grade of a C. I told Mom that Dr. Burke
suggested, strongly suggested, that I withdraw from
school, rework my portfolio for the rest of this semester
and through the summer, and then resubmit it this

coming Fall semester and do my student teaching then as well. This is all a bunch of crap, I angrily told Mom. I didn't understand any of it. How could it be that I don't comprehend all of that about teaching when I have a running GPA of 3.7 and got As and Bs in all of my courses? I told Mom that I angrily told Dr. Burke that I would withdraw from school, but that I wasn't returning, ever.

Lying is such hard work.

It all went well. Everybody believed me — Mom believed me, my sisters believed me,--Well, my sisters don't count: they don't care what I do; they're use to me, and my ways, especially Eve. — our neighbors believed me, my few remaining aunts and uncles all believed me…Well, I, actually, don't know if all of my few remaining aunts and uncles believed me, or if all of the neighbors believed me, for that matter. I have always had the belief that most of them have always viewed me as a bum, but out of respect for Mom and Dad, never voiced their true feelings of me — except for Aunt Rose, that is. She, too, is in a retirement home, and whenever she calls, which is almost every damn day, she most often as not, when I answer the phone, says: "Tom, are you at home at this time of the day? Don't you ever work?" Whenever she says this, which is often, I always want to reply: "No, I don't. Aren't you dead yet?" But I never do.

I'm a pleaser, that's what I am. I always want to please people — that's what keeps getting me into these messes, always wanting to please people. I get myself out of one mess, and then, wanting to please someone, I get myself into another mess, which often as not, turns into a bigger mess than the one that I have just gotten myself out of. This was just the case here.

So, I'm thinking about what I was going to do now,--with my life and all—and I had decided to get a full-time job;--nothing too physically or mentally demanding: perhaps in retail—get an apartment, and live the rest of my life as independently, and as peacefully, as I could. To pass the time at night, I would write, as I have always wanted to do, short stories and such. It would be a quiet life, but a peaceful one. I would read much, and write, and be a scholar of sorts. It would be a good life, I kept telling myself.

But then what happens? Everything goes topsy-turvy because of me wanting to please someone. This time, it was Mom.

I didn't think she'd take it so hard, me quitting school. But she did. She was devastated. She moped about the house, going about her daily chores by rote; she would stop repeatedly at every picture of Jesus in the house—and they're all through the house: even in the bathrooms—and say a silent prayer, which I knew was always for me, and I even caught her, at times, crying about it all. My obtaining that certification and becoming a teacher had meant so much to her. Obtaining that certification, to her, would expunge all of my past failures. Obtaining that certification, to her, would give me a second chance at life—career, money, wife, a life. It was sad. Sad, seeing her like that. I felt like such a heel.

Well, I couldn't stand seeing her like that anymore. Three days after I had told her that I wasn't going to do what the college wanted me to do, that I had quit, I said:

"You know, Mom, I guess I'm goin' to do what Dr. Burke told me to do. I'll rework my portfolio and return to school in the fall. I was just mad. I'm goin' to get my teaching certification."

She was overjoyed. She was ecstatic. She threw her arms around me and hugged me with her pudgy, little aged body,--the top of her white-haired head resting under my chin—saying: "I'm so happy. I prayed and prayed: 'Lord,' I said, 'show him the way. Show him the way.' That's what I prayed, and He has."

Yeah. Right.

Now, I had no intentions of going back to school. What I would do is stay the course, as I had decided. I'd get a full-time job;--in retail: I had worked at Famous-Barr in Ladies' Shoes once during the Christmas Holidays, and although it was hectic, I loved it. —get a crappy little apartment somewhere, and live as independently, and as peacefully, as I could. Once I had that job and the apartment, I would tell Mom that I loved my job and my life. She would be disappointed, but as long as she believed that I was happy, she wouldn't be all that upset. She'd get over it, I told myself. And anyway, my god, I'm 53-years-old. It's about time I did what I wanted to and got out of that house, right?

So, that was the plan, to stay the course.

But did any of that happen?

No.

Try as I did,--and I really did try, too—I couldn't find a job to save my soul. I read the Want Ads in the newspaper; I searched jobs on the Internet; I want job hunting every day; I filled-out application and application—no job. I couldn't find a job anywhere—and my time was quickly running out. The days turned into weeks, and the weeks turned into months, and still no job. There was only 5 weeks left until Fall semester began. Mom believed that I had everything ready to begin student teaching, because I told her I had—the portfolio, pre-registered at school, everything. All that remained to be done, I had told her, was to pay my tuition for student teaching: I told her that I could do this a week before school began. It would cost 5 thousand dollars and Mom, poor Mom, was going to take out a loan at the bank to pay for it: Poor Mom. Not only has she, and Dad, too, pay for all of my years of going to school, but we, she, lost the last 5 thousand dollars we, she, had paid for this past semester by my quitting. What a mess.

Anyway, I was beginning to panic. I just couldn't find a job. That was when, with only 5 weeks left until the Fall semester began, that Mom came rushing into the house and told me—joyously, ecstatically: The Lord had answers her prayers once again!—about Ruth and how she was going to get me a part-time job at one of the Discount Foods Stores.

My heart sank when Mom told me about Ruth and all, and I thought: Oh, shit. How do I get myself out of this one?

But I didn't. Wanting to please Mom, and not seeing any way to lie my way out of it, I accepted the job that she, Ruth, offered to me—being a part-time stocker/cashier. I say 'that she offered me' because she hired me, not Fred. I think this had much to do with his initial dislike of me. When I had the interview for the job,--which was at the store — she interviewed me and hired me. Fred sat there the whole time, silent, and looking very ticked-off. It seemed to really tick-him-off when I kept thanking her for hiring me, telling her that what with my parents being old and what with, as she knew, Dad having Alzheimer's, I didn't want to take any money from them, that having this job would help me out so much. Thanks. Thanks, so much.

I should have realized right then and there that this wasn't going to workout, that there would be trouble. But I didn't. I always live in hope that things will workout. I told myself that it was only part-time, that I would be making some money, and that I would stick with the plan and still search for a full-time job, get that apartment, and live as independently, and peacefully, as possible.

My schedule there was to be a "fixed" schedule. Mondays, Wednesdays and Fridays was when the store received its freight of groceries. On those days, I was to do freight and work from 6 a.m. to 2 p.m.; and on Tuesdays and Thursdays, I was a cashier and would work from 4 p.m. to 9 p.m. I hated both being a stocker and cashier, but doing that freight was just too physically demanding on this 53-year-old, 5-foot-7, 140-pound, out-of-shape, aged man. Ten to 12 pallets of groceries, mountainous-tall, wrapped tight in wafer-thin, see-through paper; pulled by hand from the back of the store with pallet-jacks; conveyed to their designated areas; wrap cut away with box-cutters; unload pallets; shelf groceries; take extras to back room — mindless, monotonous, backbreaking work.

When I arrived there that first morning, he, Fred, says: "This is Tim and Paul," pointing to two tall, husky guys, who were both in their early 20s, I would say. "You'll work with Tim. I run a tight ship here. Do your work; don't goof-off; do what I tell you to do, and we'll get along fine. Here's some gloves, an apron, and box-cutters. Let's get to work." He said not another word to me the rest of the day, not even goodbye when I left, or even "You worked hard. Good job" — and get this, Ruth had told me that for 8 hours of work, one got a 15 minute break and a 30 minute lunch. Guess what I got? — ZIP. At 11:30,--after having been there for five and a half hours, and after having unloaded 5 pallets — and having had no break or lunch, and being tired, hungry and thirsty, I asked Tim when we were going to get lunch, or, at least, a break. Get this, he tells me that Fred doesn't want us to stop until the freight is done. So I worked there all damn day and didn't get a lunch or a break. Well, yes I did, sort of. After the freight was done, the three of us, at 1:40, sat in the back room on empty plastic milk cartons until our shift was done, at 2 p.m.

At 2 p.m., I dragged my exhausted ass out of there, got into my car, and drove home — wondering how I had gotten myself into this mess; wondering how I could get myself out of it; and wishing that I would just die and be done with it all.

When I got home, the first words out of Mom's mouth were: "Well, how was it?"

"Pretty rough," I replied, listlessly, slowly lowering my aching, exhausted body down onto one of the kitchen chair, and then resting my forehead down on the marble-like top—Formica, I guess: white, with black specks in it—of the kitchen table, feeling, and enjoying, its coolness.

"Oh, honey," she said, greatly disappointed and sad. "I'm sorry. But you only have—what?—a month until school starts. You can make it till then."

"Yeah," I replied.

"Why don't you go upstairs and take a long, warm bath and then have a nice nap until supper."

I did.

All through supper Mom peppered me with questions about the job: What was the work like?...What were the people like?...You worked until twenty minutes before your shift ended before you got a break—and no lunch? That's against the law. They think that they can get away with that because their not union. It's the law. They can't. At least, I think it's the law. Anyway, Wednesday, you tell them that you need a break, and a lunch.

All through this, Dad sat there quietly eating, in his own private world. From time to time, he'd return to this world for a moment and say such things as: "Worked hard. I worked for-for 60 years at-at—where did I work at? Worked hard. Hard. I-I-What did I do?"

After supper, I went up to my room, turned on my portable color TV that sits on top of my desk, got a six-pack of beer from my cache of beer that I always keep hid in the closet, flopped on my bed and mindlessly watched TV and drank warm beer and thought about what I was going to do. I told myself to just stay the course, to keep looking for a full-time job, get that apartment, and live as independently, and as peacefully, as possible. On Tuesdays and Thursdays, I didn't have to be in there until 4 p.m., so on those days, I would rise early and go job hunting: But not tomorrow, I told myself. My bones and muscles just ached too much. Hell, I didn't do it that coming Thursday either. Both of those days, I stayed in bed until it was time for me to go to work.

Before I went to bed that night, Mom prayed over me, — which I can't stand it when she does; but it gives her so much pleasure that I just can't find it within myself to refuse her — saying: "'Lord Jesus, look down upon my son, who is in need of Thy wisdom, strength and mercy. Hear us, O Lord. Say but the word, and it shall be done. Amen.' There, now, it will be better. You'll see."

Nope. It wasn't.

Cashiering wasn't as bad, physically, as doing freight, but it was rough. I have always hated working at night, so if that wasn't bad enough,--working from 4 to 9 p.m. — I got next-to-no training on how to do the damn job. I thought for sure — what with that being my first time there of cashiering, or checking, as my Mom calls it — that I would stand behind one of the other employees for the night and observe as he or she worked. But did this happen? No. It was Fred's day-off, and when I got there and told the young girl at the first cash register, the EXPRESS lane, who I was, she said that Marge, down on register 4, was going to help me. Yeah, right. She was a lot of help.

Marge was a 50-ish, street-wise, heavy-set woman, with yellowing teeth from years of chain-smoking, and had a flat-wide ass that was a regular fixture, I would say, on one of the bar stools at Joe's, which is the bar at the corner of the block: I knew of her patronage at this bar because throughout the night, she kept announcing to the world, "'em beers at Joe's are gonna taste good tonight."

After showing me the operations of the cash register,--how to open it, the keys on the key board, the monitor, the scale, the sheet above the monitor containing codes, how to process checks and food stamps, etc. — she says, walking back to her register, which was to the left of the one I was on, register 5, "Take your Close Sign off the belt and get started. If you need help, give a yell."

And give a yell I did — a lot.

Marge, I can't find a code for a 3-pound sack of potatoes!...Marge, how do you do a check again?!...Marge, her food stamp card won't process!...Marge, I can't get….

It was frustrating — and fast-paced. I mean, you had to move! My mind and body raced — with high anxiety. My whole body visibly shook like maple leaves in a strong wind. And the customers were awful, asking a thousand questions that I didn't know the answers to: What aisle are those prunes on that are on sale?...Can I write a check and get $20.00 back?...What is the price…. The majority of them were low-class and poor: Food stamps and food stamps were used. It was awful.

I kept calling on Marge for help. But then, about two hours into the shift, she, I guess, got tired of my pleadings for help, and says: "Hon', this ain't rocket science. You ain't payin' attention to your screen. It tells

you what to do 99 percent of the time. Keep watchin'
your screen…You're gonna be a teacher?"

Well, after her saying that to me, I felt embarrassed,
stupid, and, yes, angry. So, after that, I only asked her for
help when it was absolutely necessary — when a customer
would begin yelling at me for taking so long, or when I
made a mistake that I couldn't figure out how to correct,
or such.

By the time the shift was over, I was drained, —
physically and mentally — and I kept thinking, dreading,
how I had to be back in there at 6 a.m. the next morning
and do that back-breaking freight again.

I hated everything — that job, my lies, my life. I just
wanted to die — and I almost got my wish, too, that night.
No sooner had I unlocked the front door of our house and
had stepped in the small, narrow, wood-floor hallway,
when I was immediately met by the long, heavy, cold,
dull, steel blade of a bayonet thrust to my stomach, its tip
but inching away from piercing my body.

"Dad! Dad!" I shouted. "It's me! Tom! Tom!"

"Oh," he said, lowering the bayonet and then
sheaving it. "I thought you was a burgerman."

"I told you before," I said to him, tired, but much
relieved that I hadn't been stabbed. "There's no such
thing as a bogyman."

"Oh, yes there is," he said. "They come in the night,
crawlin' on their bellies with rifles. You can only see
them when the night explodes with bombs and lights the
sky like day. But by then, it's too late. By then, they're on
top of you."

"Where's Mom?" I asked.

""Takin' a bath," he replied, turning around a bit and pointing to the old wooden stairs that are against the inner back wall that separates the living room and dinning room from the kitchen and laundry room: Opposite the staircase, at the edge of the bottom step of the staircase, is the door-less, arched, entrance to the kitchen—old houses are goofily built. To get to the dining room, which is to the left of the house, facing the street, you have to walk down a narrow, arched, alcove beyond the stairs; and the dinning room is all enclosed, with two large old wooden French doors that retract into the walls. But the small living room,--which is to the right as you enter the house—is all open. It has always seemed to me that the living room should be where the dining room is and vice versa.

Anyway, Mom was taking a bath because she had given Dad a bath. I knew this because his salt-and-pepper hair was still wet and he was clean-shaven. Because of his Alzheimer's, Dad, of late, has been having "accidents in his pants," and he has forgotten how to wipe himself. Mom finds the cleaning of him so disgusting that often after cleaning him she feels compelled to take a bath herself.

Mom wanted to re-warm supper for me, but I didn't want any part of that. I told her that I was too exhausted, that, no, the job had been no better tonight than it had been yesterday, that I had to get up at 5 a.m. to be in there at 6 a.m. to do that back-breaking freight, and that all I wanted to do is go to bed: I would, though, once I got up in my room, drink three, or four, beers before I want to sleep.

Before we all went to bed that night, Mom prayed over me again, and then said: "It will be better tomorrow. You'll see. Have faith in God's power."

"Hope so," I replied.

It wasn't.

It was the same as it had been Monday, and Thursday was the same as it had been Tuesday — it sucked. But, now, come Thursday night at the end of the shift, there was one difference — I had had it. I walked out of there Thursday night telling myself that there was no way in hell that I was ever coming back there.

Well, not only was that son-ve-a bitch, Fred, rude to me off-and-on throughout the shift,--whenever I made a mistake, or such — but at the end of the shift, after he had counted down my draw and tallied all of figures I had given him, he says, real sarcastically, and parroting what that fatass Marge had said Tuesday night: "You totaled your checks wrong — and you're goin' be a teacher?"

That did it for me, I'll tell you. I had had it.

Sitting at the kitchen table, eating a bologna sandwich that Mom had made for me,--with some potato chips, a pickle and a glass of milk: a quick meal so that I could get to bed fast because I had to get up so early — I said: "Mom, what am I goin' do? Doing that freight is just too hard on my back. I'm too old and out-of-shape to do it."

"I know," she sighed, sitting across from me in her robe and slippers, sipping on a cup of instant, decaffeinated coffee that she had boiled the water of in the tea kettle on top of the old stove. "I know," she repeated.

"If only I didn't have to do that freight," I said. "Checkin' isn't all that bad. But I just can't do that freight."

"Then tell him," she said. "Tomorrow go in and tell him that it's too hard on your back. Be truthful with him. Tell him that you'll gladly check, but doin' freight is too hard on your back. This way, you'll still have a job there and you won't have to do freight. He might understand. I'll speak to Ruth about it when I see her Tuesday."

"But what if he says no?" I said.

"Well, if he says no, then say: 'I'm sorry. But doin' freight is just too hard on my back.' Quit. But, it won't come to that. Let me pray over you now read hard." After getting up from the chair, she comes over and places her hands on top of my head, and begins praying over me: "'Lord, you know my son's....'"

I was both shocked and relieved by Mom's giving me permission to quit: Shocked, because Mom has never wanted me quitting jobs. I remembered how my quitting jobs began upsetting her so, that each time I quit, she started screaming at me.

"You quit again?! Oh, Thomas. You have got to stop doin' this. You're goin' to get a bad work record."

Then, I started telling her that I got fired —I was too slow…The company's downsizing…The guy said that I make too many mistakes…..

Over the years, it went from her screaming at me for quitting, to her shaking her head and believing my lies and saying: "Poor Thomas. He has such bad luck."

My quitting jobs never seemed to bother Dad. Whenever I'd feel bad about it,--mostly because it upset

Mom so much—and would tell Dad that I don't know why I keep doing it, he'd always say things like: "Well, Tom, you ought to stop quittin' jobs like that. You need money. But, I'd say, once you find a job you really like, you'll stop quittin'."

Mom's giving me permission to quit had relieved me because it gave me an out: I mean, I was more than sure that he, Fred, would fire me the moment I told him that I couldn't do that freight—and I was right, wasn't I? Because that's just what he did. He fired me, right? Even if I had intended to tell him that I'd stay if he'd permit me to continue checking,--which I had no intentions of doing—he didn't even give me a chance to do that, right?

Anyway, actually, the only lie that I told Mom was that I had physically gone in there, to the store, and had told him that doing that freight was just too hard on my back. No, the next morning, I got up at 5 a.m.,--was as quiet as I could be: not wanting to wake up Mom or Dad—washed and dressed and got ready for work. Then, I went downstairs, made some coffee, and then had some; then, at 20 to 6, I called him, Fred, and had that conversation with him, in which he, in so many words, fired me and threatened me. Then, I left the house, went to a restaurant and had a big, enjoyable breakfast. About 2 hours later, I returned home and told Mom—me feeling all sad and depressed about the whole situation—about what he had said, that he didn't even give me a chance to tell him that I would still check, still be a cashier. He just fired me. Poor me.

Now, I had worried about getting caught lying—the other shoe falling—when Mom would speak to Ruth the following Tuesday at their prayer meeting,--that Fred would have told Ruth that I had called and quit and that Ruth would tell Mom that I hadn't gone in there, that I had just phoned him and quit—but I hadn't need worry about that at all. When Mom told Ruth that Fred had fired me, she replied: "He's better off not working there. It's a lousy company to work for." That's all that was said about me. Ruth had too many of her own problems that she wanted to cry on Mom's shoulder about to care about me. That same day I had quit, by the end of that day, Ruth herself had been fired. Besides that elderly man that Fred had accosted calling the police to have Fred arrested, he, that elderly man, was threatening to sue the company. The owner of the company, of those 4 stores, felt that Ruth had shown "poor judgment" in keeping tabs on the work and the personalities of the managers of those stores and fired her.

So I had missed the bullet on that one—the other shoe didn't fall.

Everything turned out great. Life was good again---well, life was good again from that Friday on. I felt so good, that that Friday I went job hunting. And that weekend was so enjoyable—so restful and peaceful. I slept; I read; I watched TV; I drank beer, and on and on. It felt great. My life was back on track again—to get that full-time job, that apartment, and to live as independently, and as peacefully, and possible. Life was good again. Then, life got bad again—the other shoe began to fall again. But only this time, it was not only my life and lies that were threaten to be exposed, revealed, but death. The burgerman manifested.

It began that Sunday evening, at 6 p.m., when the calls started.

They were just calls, every hour on the hour until 10 p.m. No one was ever on the other end. When Mom or I answered the ringing phone and said Hello, it was always followed by an immediate click of the phone on the other end being hung-up. This went on for three days — from 6 p.m. to 10 p.m., every hour on the hour: The phone rings; Hello; click.

Mom said that it was just kids playing around. I told her that I didn't think it was — that kids, even teenagers, wouldn't call every hour on the hour and just hang-up. Where would be the fun in that? Those calls really began to bug me, and anger me: Once, I got so angry, that I shouted into the receiver of the phone: "Stop callin' here you piece of shit!" After a pause, I heard: "How dare you talk to me like that, Tom. You have no right tellin' me that I can't call. It's not your house. You don't pay…." It was Aunt Rose.

I told Mom that we should change our telephone number and get an unlisted one, but she was adamantly against doing that: Oh, no. We've had this number for as long as I can remember. A new number would be too hard for your aunts and uncles to learn, what with them being old and living in retirement homes or with their children — and what about all of the people in my prayer groups? There's just too many of them to give a new number to. No, that would just be too difficult. It's just kids. They'll stop once they tire of it. Mary and Eve, my sisters,--both of whom live in different states — wanted us to get Caller ID, but Caller ID wouldn't even work on that old phone of ours: It's just an old black phone that sits on top of a small wooden stand in the kitchen, almost next to the door-less entrance of the kitchen. It doesn't even have an answering machine to it. It's that old…I'll tell you, everything in this house is old — the house itself is old, the people in it are old, the furniture is old,--late 1950s stuff — the atmosphere is old, and the very air we breathe in here is old. About the only modern conveniences that we have are the small microwave in the kitchen and the VCR that sits on top of our old, wooden-framed,--mahogany stained — colored TV in the living room: Mom still can't work that VCR, no matter how many times I have shown her how to. Oh, and I tell a lie: My computer, here on top of my desk, is another modern convenience that we have. I'm even on the Internet.

Anyway, by Tuesday night, I had had it with those calls. I told Mom that I was taking Eve's advice and calling the phone company the next day. Eve had told me that the phone company could put a trace on all of our in-coming calls and then send us a printout of them. Having that printout, we could then determine who was calling us and pass that information on to the police. Then, at exactly 10 p.m. on the hour, the other shoe fell: He spoke.

"Are you watching your back?" he said. That's all he said, and then, click, he hung-up. I-I froze. I mean, I-I started shaking — my whole body started shaking, with fear. I was so scared that I — well, I peed in my pants, a bit. I immediately recognized his voice. My mind raced. I kept shouting, silently: Oh, my God! Oh, my God! Why is he callin' me?! What does he want?! Oh, my….

I wanted to run. I wanted to hide. I wanted to call the police. I wanted my mommy and daddy.

Mom was upstairs, giving Dad a bath. In a daze, I want into the living room and sat down upon our long, old couch. I didn't know what to do. I stayed down there until a little after midnight, waiting for him to call back. He didn't.

Needless-to-say, I didn't get much sleep that night—not even the drinking of four beers helped. Throughout the night,--besides being plagued with trying to figure out why he was doing this to me, and what I could do to get him to stop—I kept getting up and peeking out the window on the darken street and sidewalks below, looking for him, for Fred. He was never there, though. But I'll tell you, I slept that night with all of the lights ON,--the ceiling light and the standing lamp next to my bed--and with my baseball bat, which is usually kept under my bed.

The next day, although sleepy, my fear of Fred had been expunged by the power of the sun—well, at least with it being day, I wasn't as afraid of him as I had been the night before, what with it having been so dark and all. I told myself that maybe now he wouldn't call anymore, that, OK, now he has made good on his threat, right? He was trying to scare me, right? Well, he had accomplished that. I'll admit it. He scared me. So maybe now, he wouldn't call anymore, right?

Nope.

For the next two nights, every hour on the hour, from 6 p.m. to 10 p.m., "Are you watching your back?" Click.

What a mess. I didn't know what to do. I was all alone. I couldn't tell anyone that I knew who it was — what? — and have my lies revealed? Tell Mom, or my sisters, or the police that this guy was stalking me, terrorizing me, because I quit that stupid job? I should have my life, my lies, revealed for that?!

By Friday, I had had it. I couldn't take it anymore. I was a nervous wreck. Mom wasn't feeling well and went to bed about 7 o'clock. I was glad of this, of her going to bed early, because I could do what I wanted to do, which was this: I left the receiver of that damn phone off of its cradle, hiding it, with its long extension cord, behind the stand, on the floor, so that if Dad — during his nightly check of doors and windows — happened to come into the kitchen, he, hopefully, wouldn't see that the receiver was off of its cradle and replace it. From previous experience, I knew that by leaving the receiver of the phone off of its cradle, within minutes the phone would go dead. Doing that pleased me much. It was like I was sticking it to that son-ve-a-bitch. It felt good. I got a good night's sleep, and when I awoke the next morning, I felt refreshed, rejuvenated. But, boy-oh-boy, I sure paid a heavy price for having done that.

The next morning, Saturday, it was, about 11 a.m.,-- after I had gotten back home from the dentist — he called — and was he angry.

"You turned off the phone last night, didn't you, prickface?" he said. "Don't lie to me, prickface, see. You're in enough trouble."

"Yes, I did," I replied, sheepishly.

"Don't you ever do that again, see," he said. "If you ever do that again, I'll be right over. Got it."

"I'm-I'm sorry," I said, sheepishly, "really, I am. "Listen," I then said, sheepishly, real sheepishly, "what's this all about? What do you want? What can I do to end this?"

"Well, last week I wanted you to do the manly thing and come into work," he said. "But you chose not to do that, didn't you? You chose not to do what I told you to do. See, you, like that bitch wife of mine, thinks that you can waltz through life doin' whatever you please and there's no consequences to your actions. Well, prickface, you, like her, are wrong. I'm the teacher now, and you're goin' to learn from me. And 'What's this all about?' and, 'What can you do to end it?' — nothin'. See, I got three bullets with names on them. The first bullet has my bitch wife's name on it; the second bullet has your name on it, and the thir — "

"My name?!" I said, interrupting him, shaking with fear. "Look, Look. This is goin' too far. I'm very sorry for what I did. Please forgive me — and-and, if you would do such a thing like that — to your wife, or me, you'll be arrested for murder. You might even be exec — "

"So what," he said. "See, I'm already dead. I don't give a shit anymore. If people would have only done what I told them to do, none of this would be happenin'. Consequences, baby. See, first, I'll kill that bitch wife of mine for runnin' off again with my kids when I told her that if she ever done that again, I'd kill her; — I'll find her. I'll find her. She's got to be in Columbia — Columbia, Missouri; that's where she's from. I'll find her. — then I'm goin' kill you for—well, just for fun, really. You really pissed me off that day. See, you're like the straw that...."

On and on he went. It was horrible. I bet he talked for about an hour. He was living on the run. There was a warrant out for his arrest for what he had done to that elderly man. Towards the end of that conversation, he told me not to worry about him killing me, that he still had to find his bitch wife first. Plus, he wasn't totally resolved to killing her before he killed me. Much of that decision would have to do with "logistics." When I asked him—real sheepishly—wasn't he concerned that I'd call the police and tell them about all of this and have them place a wiretap, or something, on the phone to catch him, he replied: "No. See, you're gutless, just like that bitch wife of mine. You won't do that. Your kind doesn't like confrontation. You'd rather make excuses, or apologize, or take the back door, or run home to mommy and daddy. See, you...."

He liked to talk, I'll give him that much. And so, our conversations began, our relationship began.

The only redeeming factor in this burgeoning relationship of ours was that the calls became less—not on the hour every hour from 6 p.m. to 10 p.m. The calls still came between the hours of 6 and 10 p.m., but there were never more than two or three calls per night. The calls were longer, though, which displeased me much. A couple of times that son-ve-a-bitch talked for well over an hour. Unfortunately, I think I got to know the son-ve-a-bitch pretty well—his views, opinions, and beliefs of life, the people in it and himself. And he was one mess-up guy, too. He was anti-social; saw life with no shades of gray;--you were either right or wrong; his friend or enemy — racist; narrow-minded; and had the mind-set of a Hitler.

It was horrible. Night after night, I sat there at the kitchen table with the receiver of the phone to my ear, listening to him talk. He always did 99 percent of the talking, with me interjecting a "yes" here and a "no" there. The conversations ran the gamut from his childhood, life, philosophy of life, to politics, religion, and sex. Now, that was one conversation that had disturbed me — that one about sex. When we had had that conversation, about sex, I think he had been extremely lonely — and drunk.

"I like it hard, Tom," he said. "The harder, the rougher, the sex is the better. I like it...I broke that bitch wife of mine's ribs twice havin' sex. Well, it was her own damn fault. See, if she had listened to me and had done what I told her to do, it wouldn't have happened. But, no, she always had to fight me. 'You're hurtin' me! Stop! Please stop!' Well, boo-who-who. If she was here right now, I'd make her get down on her knees, unzip my pants, and — Are you a homo, Tom?"

"No, I'm not," I said.

"But you don't know women, do you?" he said. "You've never known the power and passion that comes from being the man with a woman do you? See, that's a man's job. Women are the weaker...."

It was horrible.

I hated those calls. It's odd to think that such a seemingly innocuous thing as the ringing of a telephone can suddenly be equated with watching the executioner pulling the switch of the electric chair you are sitting in.

I got a much welcomed, and needed, reprieve from his calls last Sunday, though. He called about 7:30 that night, but the connection was bad. After he said: "Tom…Tom," I heard him say: "F-ing cell phones." Then, he was no longer on the line, and he never called back. I was so thankful for that. I was tired of being his bitch wife.

When he called Thursday, he was jubilant, ecstatic, drunk with both drink and joy: He had found her, his bitch wife. All of his "leg work", and his driving to Columbia, Missouri,--which is about a 100 miles west of St. Louis, I would say — almost every day for the past two weeks had paid off. He should have been a private detective, he had said, arrogantly, adding that "women are so stupid." He was copious with the details of how he had found her.

Towards the end of that conversation, I mustarded up enough nerve to ask him if he was still going to kill her, and if so, when? He responded with a deep belly laugh — the first true laugh that I had ever heard come out of him.

"What's the matter?" he then said, still laughing. "You gettin' nervous about when I'm goin' to kill you? Soon. Soon," he said. "See, I want it to come as a complete surprise to her, but I also went to spend some 'quality time' with her. She, like you, has to learn about consequences. It's the same with my kids. 'Can't you see how scared they are of you?' she'd say. Good. They should be scared of me. That's respect. I'm teachin' them respect—and consequences. I'm teachin' the boy that it's his job to be a man, and the girl that it's her job to please a man. I'll teach them. I'll teach them all. When I'm done, people will remember me. When I'm done, the whole god-dam…."

God, it was horrible. Simply horrible—listening to his vile ramblings night after night. His phone calls were beginning to take their toll on all of us. Every time the phone rang, Mom and I would jump with fear, and Dad would shout: "Burgermen! Burgermen! I'll kill them!" Mom was beginning to look as if she had aged 10-15 years in the last two weeks. The involuntary rocking of her head to and thro had increased 10-fold, and was lessoned only by the placement of her hands to the sides of her face. From 6 p.m. on, I wouldn't permit her to answer the phone anymore: I had told her that maybe by my speaking with him, I could get him to stop calling. But Mom was beginning to crack-up from the strain that she knew it was having on me. Friday, while I was on the phone with him, in a fit of rage, Mom grabbed the receiver of the phone from my hand and shouted into it: "Who are you?! What do you want with us? Leave us alone. This is a house of God. You got the devil in you. In the name of Jesus, I rebuke the devil in you. Devil, come out!" Then, she slammed down the receiver of the phone on its cradle, confident that it was finally over: He would not call back. No more than a 5-count after Mom had slammed down the receiver of the phone, it rang again. In all honesty, I can't tell you if she was more disappointed that it was him calling again, or that her exorcism of the devil in him had failed. After she had answered it, with much disappointment, and anger, she handed me the phone and said: "Here. He wants to speak with you."

By Sunday, we had had it. We couldn't take it anymore—nerves were at the breaking point; the anxiety; the pressure; the fear; a simple word said; a simple act done, if taken wrongly, would be enough to send us into atavism.

Because of all of us having trouble getting to sleep at night, we were sleeping late into the day, and that Sunday was no exception.

About 10 minutes after ten o'clock, Mom comes dragging herself into the kitchen, looking tired and worn-out. I was sitting at the kitchen table, drinking a cup of coffee and dreading the fact that she would want to go to twelve o'clock mass. I felt tired and depressed and disconnected, and I didn't feel like dealing with anything, or anybody.

"Do you want some oatmeal and toast?" she asked, pouring herself a cup of coffee.

"I don't want any goddamn oatmeal or toast," I said.

"What did you say?" she said, turning around and facing me. "Don't you ever use the Lord's name in vain in this house—especially on the Lord's Day."

"I will if I goddamn please," I replied. "I'm sick and tired of livin' in this goddamn—"

"Stop it! Stop it!" she shouted. "In the name of God, stop it!...That's it," she then said. "That's it. I'm not livin' like this anymore. We're prisoners in our own house. Look at you—you don't eat; you don't sleep; you

don't leave the house anymore. All you do is wait for
him to call. It's over. When's that printout of our calls
comin' from the phone company? You said that they told
you it would be here in a few days. Where is it? What's
their number? I'm callin' them myself, today — and
you're not talkin' to that guy anymore. That's out."

"I have to," I said.

"Why?" she asked.

"I told you before," I said. "My thought is that by
speakin' to him, I can get him to stop callin' here."

"Well, it's not workin', is it," she replied. "No.
You're not talkin' to him anymore."

"I have to," I said.

"Why?" she said.

"Because I have to," I replied.

"Why?" she repeated.

"Why?! Why?! Why?!" I shouted. "It's always
'Why?!' with you. You're always in my business. I'm
sick of it! I can't take it anymore! Why, why, why...You
want to know 'Why?!'" I continued. "I'll tell you 'Why?!'
"Because he said that if I don't answer his calls, he'll come
right over here and kill me...He's goin' to kill me! The
other shoe's fallin'. He's goin' to kill me...Kill me! Kill
me!" I kept shouting as I pounded the palms of my
clenched fists down hard on top of the table. "He's goin'
to kill me!" Then I burst into tears.

"Oh, honey," Mom said, rushing over to me. She
took me in her arms and I turned around and wrapped
my arms around her and buried my head in between her
breasts.

"There, there," she said. "He's not goin' to kill you. He's just a nut. Why on earth would he want to kill you? You don't even know him."

"Well," I said, separating from her and wiping away the tear from my eyes and face, "he says that about two weeks ago, I cut him off the road and he followed me home to beat me up. But then, he decided to kill me."

"Oh, he's not goin' to do that," she said. "If he was goin' to kill you, he would have done it by now. He's just a bully—a coward; and cowards don't hurt anybody."

And by golly, she was right. The moment that those words left her mouth and entered my ears, it struck me for the first time like a punch in the face: He was a coward. I mean, if he was such a tough guy, what was with all of those phone calls, and with all of that time passing? Why didn't he just come over and kill me? —or his wife? Logistics, my ass. The coward!

"You're right, Mom," I said. "He's nothin' but a coward. But I do want this to be over. Mom, why can't we just get a new phone number, an unlisted one? Then, this would all be over. Peace would return to this house."

"Do it," she said. "Call the phone company right now and do it."

It was great. Just great. I felt as if the weight of the world had suddenly been lifted from my shoulders. I was finally free of him—FREE of him. It was great. There was one glitch in this, though. The representative from the phone company whom I spoke with told me that it usually took about 24 hours before the new number would be activated. But, under the circumstances,--what with some guy making threatening calls, and even though it's Sunday — he assured me that he would place a "rush order" on the ticket.

This disappointed me, somewhat, because I wanted to be rid of this guy. Then Mom and I talked it over, and everything was fine after that. I told Mom how we could leave the receiver of the phone off of its cradle, and that within a few minutes, the line would go dead. I told her that this was what the representative from the phone company had told me that I could do until the new number was activated: No, no, no. Doing that won't damage the phone at all, he assured me of this. Once we replace the receiver of the phone back on its cradle, the phone will start working again. Thankfully,--Thank you, God. — Mom agreed to do that. She said that after she had called everyone she could think of and told them the situation and gave them our new, unlisted, number, we would leave the receiver of the phone off of its cradle until the next day — wouldn't use the phone at all until the new number was "activated."

It was great.

After mass, Mom cooked us a big, hearty breakfast, — eggs, bacon, buns, the works — and we all tore into it and gobbled it all up like starving wolves. It was great. We talked and laughed, and peace seemed to have return to the house.

After helping Mom with the dishing and such,--so that she could begin making her calls to everyone about our situation and all — I went up to my bedroom and spent most of the remainder of the day there — took a nap, read the Sunday newspaper, watched some TV, drank a beer, took another nap, and such.

It was great. I felt good. In fact, I felt like my old self again. I told myself that tomorrow, after I knew that our new, unlisted, phone number was "activated," I was going out job hunting. I would fulfill my epiphany. I would get that full-time job, that apartment, and begin living as independently, and as peacefully, as possible. It would be a quiet life, but a peaceful life. It would be lonely, but I'm use to loneliness, I told myself. No, it will be a good life. Hell, I might even start writing those short stories and novels that I always told myself that I'd one day begin writing.

Yes, it was a most relaxing, peaceful Sunday. Oh, sure, off-and-on throughout the remainder of the day, I had some moments when the thought of him surfaced to my conscious mind and-and disturbed my bliss, but they were only passing thoughts. I quickly brushed them off, the same way you would brushed away a nagging fly in front of your face. Except for those passing moments, as I have said, it was a most relaxing, and peaceful, Sunday. But, boy-oh-boy, after supper, with night coming, I sure started to get nervous — about him, about Fred.

I decided to stay downstairs and watch TV with Mom, in the living room. After "60 Minutes" is over, Mom usually watches whatever movie is on that follows "60 Minutes." But shortly after that movie began, I could tell that Mom didn't like it. It was a blood-and-guts movie, with that karate guy, that Steven Sugal, or Segal, or something like that. I knew Mom didn't like it, so I suggested that we watch one of her Thin Man movies: Mom likes all of those old movies from the '40s — movies with Clark Gable, Cary Grant, Spencer Tracy, and such.

She really likes those Thin Man movies, with Myrna Loy and William Powell. They made 6 of them, and two years ago,--while I happened to be in Borders one day and saw all 6 of them being sold there as a set—I bought them and gave them to Mom as a Christmas present. She just loves watching them. Watching them never fails to lift her spirits and make her laugh. I bet she's watched them over a hundred—well, she's watched them a lot.

So, that's what we did. We watched one of her Thin Man movies.

Sadly, though, Mom didn't get to watch much of it. She kept falling to sleep. All of this has taken such a toll on her—physically and mentally. Poor Mom. She didn't deserve any of this. It must be very lonely for Mom now, what with all of the people she loves—James, my aunts and uncles—dead, or near death, and what with Dad being just a dried-up shell of what he once was, and what with her children being a disappointment to—well, it's sad.

After the movie was over, I woke Mom and told her that maybe we should go to bed.

Throughout the day, I bet Mom and I told Dad a thousand times not to replace the receiver of the phone back on its cradle. Then, right before we all went up to bed, I told him again—to be sure and not replace the receiver of the phone back on its cradle. He was in his pajamas, robe and slippers, with the Army belt around his waist and the sheaf and bayonet to his right side.

When I told him this time to be sure and not replace the receiver of the phone back on its cradle, he gave me a salute, then pointed to the phone and said: "Burgermen.

Burgermen." Then he patted the sheaf and bayonet with his right hand and said: "I'll get them. I'll get them."

After taking off my jeans, shirt, shoes and socks and donning my bed clothes,--which is a T-shirt and sweat pants—and after recovering my baseball bat from underneath my bed and lying it on the bed, I went to bed—keeping the light of the standing lamp next to my bed ON.

Obviously, I didn't get much sleep. I'll admit it: I was scared. Like I had done that night when Fred had first spoken, I kept getting up every 15 minutes or so and looking out the window onto the darken street and sidewalks below to see if Fred was there. No, he was never there, but that was of little comfort to me. I was still scared. It took the drinking of 4 beers before I finally fell to sleep, which was about 1 a.m.

It was a fitful sleep, too. I kept having nightmares, and one of them, I kept having repeatedly. In it, someone, or something, kept chasing me. He, or it, never caught me, but I couldn't escape him. He, or it, always found me—no matter how fast, or far, or where, I ran. He, it, always found me. Then, the last time I had that nightmare, he spoke, for the first time. He kept calling my name: "Tom! Tom! To...."

Then, I woke up.

Groggily, I shot up in bed, hearing my name being called echoing in my ears. But then I realized that it was the phone downstairs, ringing.

I looked over at my alarm clock on top of my desk. It was 2:40 a.m.

I immediately knew what had happened: Dad, in making his nocturnal rounds of checking the doors and windows, making sure they were locked — had replaced the receiver of the phone back on its cradle.

Not wanting the ringing of the phone to wake up Mom or Dad, if Dad was asleep, that is: not making his rounds--and wanting it to stop, too! — I dashed downstairs.

It was dark downstairs, which is unusual: At night, Mom and I are continuously turning off lights that Dad continuously turns on. The only light downstairs came from the streetlamps and the moon shining through the tall, narrow windows in the living room.

I don't know when, exactly, but somewhere between the top of the stairs and the bottom step of the stairs, I became enraged. I was sick of it, and of him. I had had it, and I was going to tell him so.

After dashing into the kitchen, I grabbed the receiver of the phone and shouted this into it: "Listen you sick son-ve-a-bitch, I've had it with you. If you want me, come and get me. I'll be waitin' for you."

I was about to slam the receiver of the phone down when from it — and from the living room, I thought, too, which made me look in that direction — I heard muffled laughter, which was followed by: "You don't have to wait. I'm here." And he, Fred, stepped out of the darkness into the doorframe of the kitchen, with cell phone in one hand and a gun in the other.

I-I froze, but then, as he had stepped into the doorframe of the kitchen, I stepped back. He stood before me, 5 or 6 feet away.

"See, consequences," he said. "No one anymore thinks of consequences. I told you what I was goin' to do, but you didn't listen—you didn't do what I told you to do. Now get down on your knees and start beggin'. It's not goin' to help, but it will buy you a few minutes out of that black box of eternity. Make it fast, though. I'm drivin' to Columbia tonight."

God, if only he hadn't said that. It all might have been different. If only he hadn't said that.

"I'm not beggin' you," I said, defiantly. "You make me sick. You don't own me and you never will. What I cherish more than anything else in life is freedom. So, see, go F yourself."

"You're dead," he said. He raised and straightened the arm of the hand that held the gun, pointing and leveling the barrel of it right between my eyes. "See," he said, "consequences. No one anymore wants to—" and then I saw his left shoulder, which was the shoulder of the arm and hand that was holding the gun, jerk back a bit as if it was being pulled back. Then, he made a painful sound of "Ahhhhh." Then, his whole body went stiff, with the upper half of his body arching forward. His eyes bulged out and his mouth dropped open. It said: "No! It's not suppose to—consequences. Con—"

The body flew forward and smacked the black-and-white tiles of the kitchen floor with a dull thud. The top of his head lay at my bare feet. There was a tear in the back of the black pullover sweater he had on,--about midway up, where his ribs would begin, on the right side—and something was flowing out of the tear, making the black sweater even blacker, and wet.

"Damn burgermen," my father said, wiping blood off of the blade of the bayonet with the red handkerchief that he always keeps on him. "I got him. I got him."

Well, that's my story.

From my desk, as I gaze out of my bedroom window, I can see the sun beginning to rise, above the rooftops and the treetops, at the horizon. It's beautiful. It's like watching a baby being born — full of newness, energy, promise and hope. In some measure, I feel reborn. I don't know why I do — because nothing has changed, actually — but I do. I feel at peace and free. I'm going to tell Mom that the college couldn't get me placed in a school this semester and told me to do my student teaching the following semester. This will give me time to find something, hopefully.

It's a new day, a new beginning. But, damn, I sure hope Mom and Dad live a long, long time.

~ The End~

Lifer

by

Clint Stutts

Deon read the same Popular Mechanics issue he'd read two months before, and inwardly wished somebody in the prison's administration would make it their life's purpose to ensure that all inmates at Louisiana State Penitentiary were provided with up to date reading materials at all times. He knew it would never happen though, and he really couldn't blame them. He was a lifer, convicted of killing his wife and her lover almost ten years before. He didn't just kill them though. Oh no, he made a real mess of it. Between his wife and her lover, Deon had left over three hundred stab wounds. That's what got him the ten consecutive life sentences without the possibility of parole. The funny thing was that he didn't remember any of it. Deon was thirty seven now, so he figured he'd make it through about two and a half of those life sentences before he died. That was only if he was lucky.

Deon's bunkmate, Jerry Pangborn, was another lifer, but not because of cold blooded murder. Jerry was a child molester, and had been quite busy before he was finally caught. By the time Jerry's day in court came around, twenty seven victims, all boys, had come forward to testify against him. Jerry was handed down twenty five life sentences, with no possibility for parole.

Deon was paired with Jerry because the warden and the guards all figured Jerry was the least likely to kill the pervert. Anybody who knew Deon knew he really wasn't a killer, he just flipped out for about an hour ten years ago. They also knew he had an idiot attorney who couldn't even get him off on an insanity plea. That was just the way things played out for poor black folks in the south, Deon supposed. Deon understood well enough that he had murdered two people, and he grieved for what he'd done, but deep down inside he knew he'd never be capable of it again.

Deon got along with Jerry most of the time. They even had some good conversations about such things as politics, religion, fast cars, and the good old days of their youth. Sometimes, though, Jerry wasn't all there. This usually happened when he looked at a picture of a little boy he'd torn out of a magazine some months ago. He'd sit and stare at that picture for hours without saying a word or moving at all. It was during these times Deon felt sure he was seeing the real Jerry, and right now was one of those times.

"Jerry, you okay down there?" he asked. No response came from the bottom bunk.

"Alright then, I'll leave you alone."

Deon shut his magazine and threw it toward the foot of his bed. He jumped down to the floor and eyed the toilet in the corner of the cell. He really had to take a dump, but Jerry's gaze was toward the toilet. Deon knew Jerry was actually looking at the picture, but still…

"Hey Jerry, you mind turning around or something? I gotta take a crap." No answer, no acknowledgement, nothing. "Geez, man, at least lay down and stare up at my bunk or something. I don't wanna go with you looking my way like that. It gives me the creeps."

Jerry suddenly snapped out of his coma and locked eyes with Deon.

"I have to tell you something," he said, his voice quivering.

"So? Say it so I can take a crap."

"I met this boy today. I know it sounds crazy, but I really met him today. He lives in Cooper, Alabama, just like the photo caption says. I swear to God man, I met him. Why are you looking at me like that?" Deon's clean shaven face showed a look of concern for Jerry.

"I'm looking at you like this because you haven't left my sight all day long. You've been spaced out for about two hours now, looking at that picture. I just hope you didn't molest that poor boy in your mind."

"No! No, you got the wrong idea. Yeah, I have those kinds of thoughts, but I won't act on them. Swear to God I won't. But you gotta believe me. I was there, Deon. I talked to him, shook his hand, and wished him luck."

"Wished him luck for what?" Deon asked.

"In his baseball game. His team was playing in a tournament today. He's the first baseman."

"Man, you've got yourself an overactive imagination. If I had an imagination like yours, I wouldn't miss T.V.," said Deon.

Jerry grimaced. "Please, you have to believe me. Have I ever lied to you before?"

"Not that I know of," Deon replied.

"Then just listen to what I have to say." Deon sat on the toilet lid opposite Jerry. He wore an impatient look on his face. "Go ahead, I'll listen," he said.

"I've been looking at this picture for months now, and you've even told me that I space out when I do it. You say I don't talk or move or anything. That's because I'm not here. And I'm not talking about my imagination, either. When I'm spaced out, I'm hovering like a spirit over the location in this picture."

He held the page out to Deon so he could see it. Deon judged the boy in the picture was about ten years old. He was dressed in a baseball uniform, and a baseball field was behind him.

"It's always the same day when I'm there. I don't know what the month or year is when I'm there, I just know I travel to the time and place in the picture. This little boy's team is always playing a game, and it's a beautiful day. I usually just fly around and enjoy the air and sunshine, but sometimes I watch the little boy's game. His name is Brock Crews, and he plays first base for the Tigers. Anyway, I sometimes fly around and watch the game from a birds eye view, but today I wished I could watch it from the ground. I wished it so hard, I suddenly felt myself descending. I descended right into a guy sitting by himself in the stands. I don't know his name or anything, but I possessed that guy today. I left him after the game was over, but Deon, I think I can possess someone forever."

Deon didn't know what to think. Jerry had always been straight with him, and it sure explained a lot about his fits, but Deon was having a hard time swallowing what he'd just heard.

"I could've done it today. I could've stayed. But I came back to tell you about it so you could come with me."

"Come with you? I ain't even sure if you're going!"

"You know I'm not lying. You know I'm not crazy. We can go tonight if you want. We can leave this place forever and have new lives."

"But what makes you able to leave?" asked Deon. "How do you do it?"

"It's the picture," said Jerry. "When I saw it in that magazine, I somehow knew there was something special about it. I don't have special powers or anything, and you don't need them either. All you have to do is look at the picture with me and just want to be there."

"What happens to us if we stay in Cooper forever? What about our bodies here?"

"We won't need them. We'll have different bodies. We'll just want to make sure to possess somebody who's at the baseball field by themselves. And after the game, I think we have to leave town and start new lives. It would be impossible for us to live that person's life without sticking out like a sore thumb."

Deon nodded. He wasn't skeptical anymore. Jerry was a perv, but he'd always been open and honest with Deon. If it worked, that'd be wonderful. If not, he'd just have more of the same right here in his cell, and he'd have confirmation that Jerry had a few screws loose.

"Let's do it," said Deon. "Let's get out of here."

Deon's need to relieve himself was pushed to the back of his mind. All he cared about at the moment was getting free of the place that had held him for so long. No matter how crazy the idea sounded, even the smallest glimmer of hope was enough to get Deon on the bandwagon. Deon got up from the toilet seat and sat down beside Jerry.

"I think we both need to have our hands on the picture for this to work," said Jerry. Deon grasped one side of the page with his right hand. "Now," said Jerry, "look at it and wish you were there. When you find a person to possess, just wish real hard that you can do it and it'll happen. When that happens, just stand up where you are and I'll come find you."

Deon looked and wished, and suddenly he had a feeling that was disturbing at first, then comforting. He was flying, as if in a dream, over a green field that must have been the park in the picture. The baseball field was a short distance away, but Deon could see people were sitting in the stands and the teams were either warming up or already playing a game.

Deon tried to look at himself, but he had no body. He could feel that his limbs were there, but they were invisible, or simply insubstantial. Everything was controlled with his thought. If he wanted to steer himself in a particular direction, he simply thought about it and it happened.

As he got closer to the stands, he could see several people who were sitting by themselves. One individual stood out from the others. It was a man in his middle forties, and in great shape. He looked to be the type that worked out frequently, as his muscles rippled through his red t-shirt. Deon decided he'd like to be in good shape in his new life, so he wished to possess him.

Suddenly, he felt like he was falling uncontrollably, and he fell right on top of the man he wished to possess. When he opened his eyes and looked down at himself, the fantastically fit person he had admired from above was now him. It was his body now. Deon felt around in the pockets of his new body, and found a wallet in the back left pocket of his blue jeans. He looked at the ID contained inside and found that he'd possessed Hugh Perry, age 43. Hugh Perry was also loaded, as Deon found out when he checked the cash pocket of the wallet. It contained four hundred-dollar bills, a few twenties, some ones, and three uncashed checks that amounted to just over seventy thousand dollars. A cache of business cards in one of the other pockets in the wallet revealed that Hugh was the owner of a major contracting company called Perry Construction. Son of a gun, thought Deon. I couldn't have picked a better guy to possess.

Just then it occurred to Deon that he'd forgotten all about Jerry. He looked all around the stands trying to see if anyone was standing up. Sure enough, Deon spotted a half bald guy with a beer gut standing up about two sections over. Deon stood up and looked directly at who he supposed was Jerry. The man waved at him after a few seconds and beckoned him to come over. Deon obliged and picked his way through the half full stands to where Jerry was.

"I told you it would work," said Jerry, and Deon was surprised by the voice. He was used to Jerry's throaty high pitched voice, but this guy was definitely fit for singing bass in a choir.

"It worked like a champ, man," replied Deon, smiling like an idiot.

"We're free forever," said Jerry. "We never have to go back. All we have to do is live. By the way, my new name is Dave Price. What's yours?"

Deon told him, and as he did he noticed a woman sitting several rows down who was looking at them queerly. Deon realized they had been talking too loud.

"We might want to cool it for now," he said. "Let's just sit down and watch the game. I haven't seen one in years." Jerry nodded his agreement and they sat down to watch the rest of the game. The Tigers and the Dolphins were playing, and the Dolphins were getting nailed to the wall.

When the game was over, the two newly freed men began making their way out of the stands when one of the boys on the Tiger's team began running toward them and yelling, "Dad! Hey Dad, did you see me?"

Neither of the men knew exactly what to do, and the faces of both registered looks of surprise and confusion. "Dad," the boy yelled again, "did you see me catch that ball?" The kid was almost to them now, and neither Deon nor Jerry had made the slightest move to acknowledge him. They just stood there with stupid looks on their faces. When the boy finally reached them, however, he threw his arms around Jerry. Deon felt relieved at first, but then an overwhelming feeling of dread came over him. Child molester, he thought. Jerry is still a child molester.

"Did you see the catch I made, Dad?" the boy asked again.

Jerry smiled and answered, "I sure did son, and I'm so very proud of you." Jerry reached down and picked up the young boy and gave him a huge hug. Deon felt sick just watching.

"Let's go home and tell Mom how bad we beat the Dolphins!" the boy cried. Jerry smiled again as he took the boy's hand and the little boy pulled him toward the parking lot. Jerry had apparently forgotten all about Deon.

"Hey, Dave, wait a sec," said Deon. Jerry turned around, his eyes glazed over. He was in heaven now. He just needed someone to pinch him, and Deon planned on doing the pinching. "Can I talk to you alone for a minute?" asked Deon. Jerry told his new son to wait for him in the stands while he spoke to his friend, and the kid obeyed. Deon guessed the kid's father was a good one, and he suddenly found himself feeling guilty for stealing the new body he had. Did Hugh Perry have a wife and kids? Was he a good father? Could his family get along without him? He found himself fighting back tears of grief and shame. Jerry interrupted his train of thought.

"What's up, Hugh?" he asked. "I've got a family to get home to, ya know. Probably got a big dinner waiting for me, judging by my ample layers of fat."

"That isn't what we agreed on, and you know it. We're supposed to leave town and start new lives. That was the deal."

"Things change, my friend. I like what I have here, so I think I'll stick around for awhile."

It took every ounce of restraint Deon had not to punch him at that instant. "And just what the hell do you think you're going to do? Work this guy's job and manage his family? You don't even know your wife, much less your son. They'll know something isn't right pretty quick. No, we need to go, and now."

Jerry's smile faded. "Like I said, I like what I have here. You can just go on your merry way and do whatever you want. I'm doing what I want to do now. I'm free, remember? Nobody tells me what to do anymore."

The stands were empty of people and the parking lot was almost in the same shape, so Deon began raising his voice a bit. He didn't care if the kid heard. If Deon was lucky, the kid would get a clue and run away.

"I can't let you go home with that kid, Jerry. I just can't. I know what you'll do."

"If you think I'm gonna have my way with that kid, you're wrong. I'm never doing that again. I have thoughts, but I'll never do anything about them, swear to God."

"I don't care how much you swear to God, you're still a child molester. I'd bet all the money my new body has that you won't even make it home with him before you try something. I can't let that happen. I can't just leave you alone knowing you'll hurt that kid."

Jerry's face showed fear at first, then rage. Deon was depriving him of his pleasure, and it wasn't sitting well with him. Without a word, Jerry wheeled around and hurriedly made his way toward the boy. The kid's smile was gone and a look of worry had surfaced on his face. He knew something was wrong.

"C'mon son, we're leaving," Jerry said to him. Deon didn't think, he just ran. He was almost upon him when Jerry's head cocked and he spun around just as Deon's massive right shoulder crashed into his solar plexus. Jerry went down as the wind rushed out of him. Deon went down, too, amazed at his own strength and the success of his attack. Somewhere in the background he could hear the boy screaming for his Daddy, but Deon had to ignore it and focus on the task at hand.

Deon got back to his feet and turned toward Jerry to ascertain the damage. Jerry had managed to roll over onto his stomach. He seemed to be reaching for something in his pocket.

"Give it up," Deon said to him as he approached. When he was upon him, Jerry surprised him by lashing out with a pocketknife. A lightning bolt of pain ripped through Deon's left calf muscle, and warm blood flowed down into his shoe, soaking his sock. He fell backward, clutching the wound in his left hand while at the same time trying desperately with his right hand to prop himself back up. Jerry finally found his footing again and managed to throw himself on top of Deon.

There was pain again, this time in his upper left shoulder. Deon couldn't believe it. This fat slob is going to kill me and I'm in ten times the shape he is, he thought. Deon swung wildly with his right fist and connected with Jerry's left temple, knocking him off to the side. The knife was still stuck in his shoulder, so Deon took a deep breath and pulled it out. He looked at it as if it was something that had betrayed him, and then threw it to the ground. The pain was exquisite, but so was his anger. He kicked Jerry's face over and over again. He kicked until he was out of breath and couldn't kick anymore. Wheezing from the exertion, he collapsed next to Jerry's body and observed his handiwork.

It seemed that Deon really was capable of murder. Jerry had to be dead. His face was a bloody pulp and he wasn't breathing. Deon looked down at the wound in his left shoulder and saw that his shirt was soaked completely through. Then he heard sobs behind him. The kid had made it halfway between the stands and the scene of the fight before he collapsed in fright and went into a crying fit. He'd just watched his dad get killed right in front of him. If only I'd stayed in my cell, he thought.
Deon was trying to think of something to say to him when he suddenly stopped crying and stood straight up.

Deon watched in horror as the young boy walked straight to the knife lying on the ground and then made his way to where Deon was kneeling.

"All you had to do was walk away, man," the kid said in his tiny voice.

It can't be, thought Deon. "Jerry, is that you?" he asked.

"In the flesh," he said, grinning. "Looks like you killed an innocent man. So how's that feel?"

Deon couldn't find any words to say. He'd just killed a man who'd had his whole life ahead of him. Furthermore, the body Deon inhabited was bleeding out quickly.

"I should never have brought you with me," said Jerry. You've got too much of a conscience. It's a real pity, too. We could've had some fun."

Deon managed to laugh a little. "You know, you spend several years in a cell with someone, and you think you have them figured out," he said, shaking his head.

"Don't give me that crap, Deon. You know what I am. And I know what you are, too. I listened to all your whining over the years about how you couldn't believe you could ever kill someone. Well, just look at that poor slob beside you. You're a murderer, through and through."

"But you made me do it, Jerry. You didn't give me a choice."

"Your memory sucks, Deon. I told you to walk away. You made the choice to stop me. I didn't make you do anything."

It was hard to breathe now, and the world around him seemed to be spinning. He couldn't stay in this body much longer. He wished himself out of Hugh Perry's body and he was floating again. The pain was gone and he felt healthy, as if nothing had happened. But it had all happened. Deon peered downward at the scene he had left, and watched Hugh Perry fall face first in the dirt, probably dead. Jerry, from inside the kid, yelled, "You better just go back, Deon! You hear me? Go back or else!"

Deon didn't know anything else to do, so he did go back. He flew back in the direction he had come, and just as fast as he had been transferred from his body into spirit, he was back in his own body again. His hand was still clutching the picture with Jerry's own hand, and he quickly pulled away and pressed himself against the wall of the cell opposite Jerry's seemingly comatose body. Deon was suddenly grateful he'd come back before lights out. A guard would have surely raised a flap over him and Jerry's fixation on the picture. Jerry's eyes were glazed over and he was staring into the picture like it was the only thing in the world. Deon ripped the picture from his hands and tore it into a collection of pieces. Not satisfied, he picked all the pieces up off the floor, threw them into the toilet, and flushed them. He looked at Jerry again, but nothing had changed. He was there for good. Unless…

If he dies here, he thought, maybe he dies there. Deon was saddened to find himself making the choice to murder yet again. He looked around for something to use as a weapon, but of course the prison system had made sure that could never happen. Finally, Deon approached Jerry and used the only weapon he did have:

his hands. He pushed Jerry down onto the bed and wrapped his hands around his throat. It took a few moments for him to begin squeezing. It didn't feel right to choke the life out of someone who couldn't defend themselves. Choking back tears of shame and sadness, Deon shut his eyes tight and squeezed Jerry's throat as hard as he could. He squeezed so hard it seemed his fingers would pierce the flesh and plunge into the inner workings of Jerry's throat. Only when he was near exhaustion did Deon dare to let up. He wanted to be sure the deed was done.

Back in the park, a young boy found himself standing in front of the bodies of his dad and a stranger, and he was surprised to find that he was holding a knife. He dropped it and fell to his knees. Deep, silent sobs overcame him.

Deon knew none of this was happening. He could only hope Jerry was truly dead. Deon hadn't made any noise during the murder, so no one would know what had happened until the guard came by on his rounds. Soon, they would know what he had done, but they would never know why. Deon climbed up to his bunk and lay down on his back, pondering the events of the day. It didn't take long for him to conclude that the justice system had not wronged him. He was right where he belonged. Deon didn't look at any pictures for a long time.

A Double Edged Blade

By

Scot Hanson

Part 1

The officious clutter that ranged across the desk distracted Ronak from the half-elf's blather, even though priest was mid-crescendo on yet another forlorn plea: his real motive for inviting Ronak and Aly to share his 50-point wine in his cramped rectory. The inkstands and quills, stacks of vellum and parchment, brass seals and wax sticks left only inches of actual writing space on the desk. And the room smelled of wood that was polished more than used.

Pettiness weighed down like a net thrown over their heads. So Ronak stood up, cutting the monologue short. "Pallinon. We're returning to King's Landing. I'm not wasting another day here in Mire-town."

"You mean Mirreton, m'lord Ronak," Pallinon said. "S'truth though, I think you especially would find this rewarding."

Something rewarding would be a welcome change. The past three weeks of collecting blossoms of five-fold for healing potions, scouring the cemetery for grave-spawn, hunting down that banshee (all for the sake of scavenger's privilege and Alyonnsa's conscience) was too much. The halfling's altruism was noble and all, but her principles didn't spend well back at The Phoenix Quatrième.

Aly sipped her wine, a cheerful gleam in her eye, like she was watching Parrphi's latest melodrama.

At least someone was entertained. As long as the kid didn't start grinning (her tell for volunteering them into dangerous chores), they might make a profit. Holding his sheathed saber out of the way, he sat down again. "What reward do you have?"

"Oh! You mistake me, m'lord. I don't have the reward. Just valuable information."

Three weeks of this. The pretentious half-elf flourished hints and riddles like a sideshow magician pulling carnations from a handkerchief. A snarl pressed for release on Ronak's lips. But disciplining his orcish heritage, studying the other races of the realm, and working to fit in had served him well growing up in the city. With forced calm, he asked, "Valuable to who?"

"Don't you mean, 'To whom,' m'lord?"

The pointlessness was like a slap. But steepling his fingers together firmly made it easier to resist to-whom-ing the pompous twig out his own office window. Aly would take exception to that; she liked Pallinon, Wayfather knew why. Mimicking Pallinon's accent, he said, "You should be careful at whom you point such sharp grammar."

"Of course, you're right, m'lord," Pallinon said, waving a hand. "This legend, as I was saying, would be noteworthy to anyone curious about enchanted rapiers."

Ronak froze. Escaping Mire-town had been as simple as walking out the door a moment ago. Now the bait revealed the snare, as the Hoskinport trappers said.

Expectant silence settled over the table like a web. Aly watched him, a lock of auburn hair running free alongside her cheek. She wore the odd expression she sometimes got, a jumble of almost-smile and ocean eyes trying to pierce some fog.

An ember of interest warmed in his own heart. A magic sword could transform their work. What new assignments could they fulfill? What new fame and wealth? His sword hand flexed. Best of all, perhaps, instead of enduring the lumbering blockheads at The Phoenix reciting stale rumors about magical longswords and bewitched claymores, he could quietly draw his own enchanted blade from the scabbard. Just enough to shut them up.

But it made for a distasteful decision. Take the half-elf's bait? Or deliciously throw it back in Pallinon's face? He growled, "What kind of enchanted rapier? Out of professional curiosity."

"One like your own, if I'm not—"

"Stop." Ronak leaned forward, sliding his baldric around. He displayed the sheathed weapon in both hands. "This is a dueling saber, not a rapier."

"I'm sure such lore is beyond me, m'lord."

Happy to teach the priest something useful, Ronak pulled the steel out several inches. "Beginning with the shape of the cross-section and slight curve—"

"Shut up shut up!" Aly said, fluttering her hands over the table. "What about the magic sword, Pallinon?"

"Well, I must confess, the legends contradict one another somewhat regarding Iowenna Arkenholt's weapon."

Jaw clenched at the fact that they were suddenly on another errand, Ronak sheathed the sword with a clack. But at least they didn't have to endure more lectures. "Keep your confessions, priest. Just tell us where the crypt is and we'll handle the rest."

□

The final grave-spawn recovered from Aly's turning. It lurched back toward the narrow corridor, rasping its hunger.

Ronak pinned its right arm with his sword tip and slid to that side.

The monster struggled to follow.

His hand ax severed the neck.

The body collapsed among the others.

Thrilled at the assay of skill, Ronak stood over the corpses, surveying the chamber for more targets, breathing heavily. He ignored the wretched odor of rot, using each deep draught to subdue the orcish impulse to charge whatever was next. Even fighting at peak form, to outpace Aly would be suicide.

"We alright?" Aly asked from a safe spot farther back in the hallway. She chanted one of her strongest healing spells.

The scent of fresh water filled the air and vigor flooded back through tensed arms and legs. Taking a more dignified pose, he said, "Out-bloody-standing, Alyonnsa Springhaven."

"That wight had me worried." The residual magic glow around her sun-staff illuminated the entrance as she came forward. "And those grave-spawn? They shouldn't have recovered that fast. Something's wrong."

Remembering the duel was actually as pleasant as the healing. They had performed well, blending magic and steel into a powerful dance. "I'm not worried; I've got the best sun-slinger in King's Landing watching my back." He looked down at her with a fierce smile.

Aly started to grin too, but suppressed it and smoothed out her white tabard, tucking a fold in behind her star buckle. "Well, there are some other really devout clerics in the city. Probably more talented than me."

A glance around the quiet room showed it was clear to approach the next corridor. "Nah, you're top-notch. I think we're getting close now."

"We better be. I'm getting really worn out. And you don't have any potions left, do you?"

"One. But ten silver says this next room is the jackpot. You up for a wager, kid?"

Aly tried to camouflage worry with banter. "How about I just pay you ten and you stop calling me that? You know I'm older than you."

Hiding a smirk, he led the way between stone tables laden with dust and tapestries marred with dry rot. "But I'm bigger. So obviously you get the diminutive term. If you prefer 'rookie' though, it's all the same to me."

"Well, size is relative, Hawkbrand. So if you want me to call you 'gramps' because you're bigger than me or 'runt' because you're smaller than everybody else, it's all the same to me."

That was worth another approving smile. "Not bad, Springhaven. I'll turn you into a duelist yet."

With a jaunty step, she walked by, spinning her staff leisurely. "You can get back to me on that after you've mulled it over."

Enjoying the camaraderie, Ronak joined her to examine the next hallway. At the thirty-foot corridor, he traded saber and ax for a longbow.

"Ronak?" Aly muttered, her facade falling away.

Arrow nocked and aimed down the hall, he scanned for danger. "What do you see, kid?"

"Nothing. But I feel terrible." She crept to the corner and peered into the passageway like a rabbit ready to bolt. "This isn't a good place."

Typical Aly. But a second look usually paid well. Was there something more here?

The stone walls and floor looked the same as the previous hallways. Water droplets plipped to the floor somewhere behind them. Cold air flowed into their faces, carrying the same odor of grime and decay that had enveloped them when they first entered the mausoleum.

"Stay with me, Aly. Just like we planned: clear things out, grab the sword, then back to the sunshine and green grass."

The halfling shook her head, but clutched her staff with resolve. Patient, measured steps carried them down the hall. Rounding a corner, they saw the next entranceway lit with faint sunlight. When they reached that opening, daylight was trickling down through a small chimney, gleaming on the lid of a sarcophagus. The silver was sculpted to show a reclining woman. Just outside the light, gazing at the statue, stood a robed and hooded figure.

Aly whispered, "Ronak?"

The vile aura soaking through this heart of the tomb was astonishing, but Aly's tiny question spurred him past revulsion. She was counting on him to get her out alive, just like he relied on her to get him through each fight. So despite the gut-twisting corruption rolling off this personage, this had to be just another grave-spawn to slay. "Back me up, kid." Dropping the bow and arrow, he charged. Surviving in King's Landing had quickened his legs — a thirty-foot sprint was easy and guaranteed that surprise would be on their side.

Halfway across the chamber and two-thirds through drawing his sword, the spell hit.

Confusion, as every muscle locked up, was eclipsed by panic. Then by the floor, he was frozen in mid-stride, but momentum carried him skidding across the flagstone on his side. When he stopped, the blue-gray marble of the sarcophagus filled his view.

"Ronak!" Aly's voice echoed around the room. She delved into a chant to rain holy energy down on the robed mage. A flutter of heavy cloth sleeves undermined her words and they dwindled away. Her final, hoarse murmur was punctuated by the clatter of her staff hitting the floor.

Calling to her was impossible. The muscles in his neck and mouth were clenched as tight as his arms and legs. Her name was a strangled groan in his throat. Straining shoulders and back and hips to look around didn't shift his view an inch. The only thing visible was the end of the marble coffin, with its engraving of a robed man carrying a woman in armor, one arm supporting her legs, the other cradling her head.

Silent foreboding filled the chamber. Footsteps shuffled closer and stopped behind Ronak for a few moments. Then they went to Aly. A rough thud was followed by the metallic jangle of Aly's chain mail skidding across stone. She groaned, then mumbled in a sleep-thick voice, "Ronak? What…. Who are you?" Another kick sent her sliding again. Her squeal of pain and rage was stifled into a wordless, panicked mewing.

This bastard was going to die. As soon as this idiot half-orc could break free. With a growl, Ronak flexed and fought, trying to draw his sword or kick his legs or turn his head. The magic binding was relentless. His body was his prison.

Deathly stillness reclaimed the tomb. For interminable seconds, there was nothing but the faint whistle of a song thrush filtering down through the chimney. Finally a voice like old parchment began to rasp out an incantation.

The voice brought dread down on Ronak's chest like an ogre's heel crushing his lungs. The spell would be evocation. Something to finish them off. Seconds before fire or lightning or acid annihilated them. Straining every fiber of muscle to break the paralysis, he couldn't move an inch.

The mage stopped muttering and a gust of grave-cold air washed through the chamber.

That was bad. A chill like that meant a ghost had been summoned. Or worse. And trapped inside his own body, he was powerless to keep the creature from feeding on them. It wouldn't be as decisive as a fire blast, but death would be the same result. What could he do? There had to be a way to escape!

His arms and legs collapsed like a puppet with the strings cut.

Godsword — finally! But the flash of relief sank beneath a rising tide of apprehension. This scrawny spellcaster wouldn't dare free him unless he thought there was no threat. He untangled his limbs and looked around for Aly.

She was frozen in an awkward pose, up on one elbow, the other hand holding her stomach in pain. Her pretty features were frozen in a mask of startled anger, but her eyes could move. They showed terror. Above her, a raven-black wraith hovered, its arms stretched out for her, but not yet clawing into her soul.

Thank the Wayfather, she was okay. Sort of. Ronak sprang to his feet.

"Caution, little orc." The parchment voice came from behind him. "One rash move and my pet will destroy yours."

Taking a hostage? Then the gaunt wizard wanted something from him. They had a little leverage to work with. His saber clacked home in the scabbard and he called out, "Aly, are you okay?"

Her voice was inarticulate and fearful, but she was clearly trying to be positive.

A cataract of guilt, gratitude, and fury made it hard to keep afloat. She had bravely followed him deeper and deeper into these tombs, and now she was paying the price for his greed. That had to change. The only worthwhile reward now was protecting her from this forsaken mage. After a deep breath, he turned around.

The mage stood near the foot of the sarcophagus, blood-red robes like a foul cloud overshadowing the bright silver.

Too close. The spellcaster's presence filled the air with a pollution, with an aura of pity and scorn for Ronak's flesh. Clearly, this was no regular wizard. Here was the master of the grave-spawn they had been destroying, a necromancer powerful enough to command a wight. Despite one overpowering urge to lash out at this evil, and a second impulse to run as fast and far as possible, Ronak stood still. He straightened his clothes and armor. When he could speak without a quaver, he demanded, "What do you want, old man?"

"Arrogant, half-breed buffoon. You will refer to me as Master Zalaczar." The necromancer's voice hissed forth from the deep cowl shadowing his face, yet his attention was fixed on the statue. He shuffled even closer to the sarcophagus. The silvered lid was carved in high relief, depicting an elven woman in ornate leather armor, reclining with hands clasped at her stomach. Sunlight streamed down on her peaceful face. The necromancer rested his emaciated, leathery hands on the statue's boot and stroked the instep like he was petting a cat. "You have invaded my domain, destroyed my creations, and disrupted my rest, trespasses for which I should obliterate your pathetic life. However, that would be too light a punishment. You have also violated the sanctity of my shrine, no doubt hoping to desecrate my memorial to she who is more beloved than life itself. For that offense, you will pay exquisitely."

Guilt spiked again in his heart. Not only had his ambition lured them here, but his boastful chatter had somehow forewarned the death-mage. He clenched his jaw. The heavy blame and apologies would have to wait until he got Aly out of this crypt, safe and alive. Training from the city streets made his next step clear: brazen it out. "Looks to me, Zally, like you're clinging to your life more than hers."

"Silence! This entire complex is dedicated to her. Within this vault, I preserve her memory in brilliance. My devotions ensure that throughout the ages of the world, Iowenna Arkenholt shall never be forgotten."

That name! That was who Pallinon had jabbered about, the one with the sword. Knowing that the half-elf's legends had been right about everything else — the location of the mausoleum, the magic lock, the ghouls and ghasts — this gleaming statue now doubled in value. The elven woman with flowing hair and stern beauty must have the enchanted sword inside the marble box. Where else would a warrior keep her favored weapon? If he could just get to that blade, they might survive this disaster.

Zalaczar continued, "To answer your prior question though: what I require is your service." He shoved the sarcophagus lid with both hands, smoothly sliding it open a half foot.

Surprise and anxious energy sparked together. Jump, barrel the mage aside, scrabble through whatever remained inside the box, and grab the sword — that was the simplest route. But it would leave Aly to the wraith. Faking mild interest, he edged closer and asked, "What kind of service?"

"Glorifying the memory of Lady Arkenholt." With both hands, Zalaczar reached into the sarcophagus and reverently lifted out a sheathed rapier.

Fake interest dissolved. As did every other concern. His eyes and all his trained appreciations were captivated by the weapon's beauty. It drew him closer.

The scabbard was simple leather, but wrought with intricate patterns of leaves and graceful branches. Decorations on the ricasso looked similar to the greenery, but seemed more like script. The curve of the forward-swept upper quillon arced like a bird in flight, leading round to the sturdy branches of the d-guard, then to the pommel cap. The leather wrapping on the grip was circled in turn with twisted wire. The scent of oiled steel and leather wafted in the air, while an unmistakable imbuement also flowed round the weapon, blending power of arms and sorcery more skillfully than anything imagined. Arkenholt's sword, like her sarcophagus, glowed pristine amid the gloom and corruption.

In stunned silence, Ronak gawked. The future lay before him; the past was overthrown. The fear and shame of childhood, the scraping and struggling of youth, the penny-pinching, risk-calculating life he now led — it was all gone. Victory and fame and wealth had been molded here into graceful lines. The shining, swept hilt blurred for a moment until he blinked back the tears. There ought to be a prayer for this blade. He coveted it. Never mind the grip slightly out of line or a straight-edged sword's limited effectiveness for cuts, she was a majestic weapon. She was his.

"You appreciate this gift," Zalaczar said, still holding the sword on open palms.

Ronak nodded absently.

"Then heed the charge that comes with it."

Suspicion clouded over the reverent moment. Serving a death-mage wasn't really on his list of future accomplishments. And bards at The Phoenix all told stories about desperate bargains gone awry. But it couldn't hurt to hear the old man out. Whatever trickery would get that sword into his hand was worth it. After that, they would…negotiate. Savoring the blade once more, he said, "I'm listening."

"You will fight with this sword. You will kill. Often. At each victory, before all witnesses, you will celebrate she who made you conqueror: Iowenna Arkenholt."

Not too bad. If the cost for getting this sword was merely leading a cheer for old dame Arkenholt, hells, he would write a poem for her. No. With the honors and gold ahead, he would hire someone else to write it. He would commission the poet laureate of King's Landing to compose a ballad. And sing it for her too. A giddy smile started to form, but he refocused. "I'll do it."

"Of course, you will. First, I must prepare the sword." Zalaczar began chanting under his breath.

From across the room, a faint, pleading tone quavered.

Guilt stabbed home again. The sword's glamour had overshadowed Aly. Again. Cursing himself under his breath, he started toward the halfling, then spun back. "Godsword, release her, old man!"

"Be still, fool. Granting you this boon requires an attunement of great delicacy. Halfling dabblers have neither. Your pet is fine where she is."

Annoyance and greed and protectiveness and hatred cluttered his heart. He retrieved Aly's staff and laid it beside her, trying to ignore the wraith menacing overhead. Crouching with a hand on her rigid shoulder, he whispered, "Don't worry, kid." A smile was easy enough, but it was harder to think up something encouraging to say. "This sword is going to change everything."

Her pleading sounds were drowned out by Zalaczar's imperious command, "Come to me, little orc."

Only a little longer. Whatever condescending airs the necromancer put on, he could endure it. This would be simple compared to living in Grandfather's dilapidated villa.

The necromancer held the sword upright in one hand, exposing some of the ornate linen wrappings on his wrist. The blade was withdrawn an inch above the sheath. "The final step is to bind the sword to you."

"I don't need the sword bound to—"

Zalaczar started chanting.

"Yes. Fine then." Ignoring the ritual, Ronak dove back into studying the weapon itself.

The script on the ricasso carried down onto the blade itself, splitting around the fuller. What would Arkenholt have inscribed on her blade? Back in King's Landing, there were translators who could untangle elvish cursives. More important, what were the heft and balance of the steel? His sword hand was hungry to feel the grip and the weight.

Zalaczar droned on and on. Finally the mage raised his free hand and shaped his fingers into a series of arcane gestures. "Now be still — the blade must taste your blood."

Rejection cascaded like a landslide. "Hold up, Zally—"

"Silence, imbecile!" Zalaczar hissed, his hoarse voice echoing around the chamber. "Your preferences are void. Your life is forfeit! You belong to Lady Iowenna Arkenholt, serving her legacy as I see fit. Any resistance will cost you dearly, beginning with your little sun-caster there." In a softer whisper, he asked, "Does your tiny, over-taxed mind comprehend the situation?"

Resentment and fury boiled until his fists trembled. But here, on the verge of escaping the host of life's snares, he merely glared and muttered, "Yes."

Aly's voice rose up in a plaintive protest. Zalaczar spoke over the feeble sound. "Don't you mean, 'Yes, Master'?"

Puppet strings were all the same and were all aggravating. In the back alleys, bigger kids of all races had thought it was clever to make him to say whatever asinine phrase popped into their juvenile minds. But he had survived those games, those beatings. He would survive this too. Ronak took a long, slow breath. Play the game; take the sword; kill the mage. Repeating that litany until a measure of calm returned, he said, "Yes, Master."

"Very good, little orc." Although his face was hidden, Zalaczar had a smiling tone. "Let us complete your accolade." He unsheathed the sword and it rang like a crystal chalice. Faint radiance from the blade made the necromancer's hand a gnarled blot of ink on a pristine sheet of vellum. Zalaczar lowered the point towards Ronak. "Flesh and blood are weak-willed. Forgetful. This bonding will ensure that you fulfill your charge."

Having a deadly weapon waving about his chest was irritating in its own right, but the mage's tiresome ceremony was worse. A single sweep of the arm could brandish his own sword and beat the other aside. Except Aly was in even more discomfort, more danger. The reversal had to be quick and lethal in order to protect her. Until then … a little irritation was fine.

"Yes. As you value the halfling's life, little orc, do not move." Zalaczar lowered the blade further and stepped closer. The tip hovered near Ronak's left thigh. "For our purposes, the primary channel of blood in your upper leg will be the perfect location for this curse."

Curse? The word brought a feeling of things spiraling from bad to worse. He started to lift his hands.

"Be still!" Zalaczar hissed. His breath reeked like a butcher shop's back alley. Beneath the folds of his cowl, more bandages were wrapped around his neck, but even this close only the faintest suggestion of his features was visible.

Nausea roiled upward, both from the stench and the hateful epiphany of what was happening, but that queasiness vanished at the sensation of steel touching his thigh. Cuts and worse injuries were nothing new, but that fact brought scarce comfort. It was different, being compelled to stand immobile while sharp metal was inserted into his flesh. It was obscene. Instincts to escape seethed around honed reflexes to parry in first and riposte to high-four. Vertigo tugged at him too. The only anchor was Aly.

Zalaczar murmured near Ronak's shoulder, "Be still … or perish." He began to disgorge an incantation that left the air foul in scent and sound while he slowly pushed the blade home, inch after careful inch. Beside the sound of fabric tearing, the blade penetrating skin and muscle only made a faint, moist whisper.

Godsword, it burned. Like acid. Ronak winced. He gasped and shifted weight off that leg. Warm blood trickled, then flowed faster down his knee. The natural response to reach down and stop the flow of life escaping the wound was thwarted by unyielding steel still buried there. And the necromancer wouldn't hesitate to kill. To keep Aly alive, he had to stay alive. So he endured. Forcing slow breaths barely countered the tight panic rising in his chest.

Zalaczar's chant seemed to feast on the pain, but also inflame it like a bonfire. Even when he withdrew the blade, the cut seethed with preternatural agony. At last the necromancer stepped back a pace and proffered the weapon's hilt. "Your sword, valiant servant of Lady Arkenholt."

In a frisson of despair, Ronak grabbed it. Then he collapsed. Keep the weight off his bleeding leg; get it healed. One hand pressed on the cut, trying to staunch the blood and causing a flare of corrosive pain. It forced another groan, but he held the wound tight. He released the sword and scrabbled through his knapsack for a healing potion. Once the cut was knitting back together, the old man would regret everything. Everything!

"Yes, very wise," Zalaczar said as if he were complimenting a child. "Attend to the most urgent matters first. If you bind the incision skillfully enough, it might be several days before you need to replenish."

Cold rejection of the necromancer's words made a good focus against the pain. With the last potion in hand, he bit the stopper and tore it free. Red slurry splashed over the wound and its cool balm banked the fire. Yes. Rejuvenation would fill him like a spring tide and then he would pierce the necromancer's heart with this same blade. He guzzled the rest and a wash of invigoration swelled throughout his head and chest and arms. It energized one leg, but left the other still aching abominably. A glance showed that the cut wasn't closing; blood kept seeping from the dissevered flesh. Ronak clutched at it again, gritting his teeth and raging. "Zalaczar! What did you do to me?"

"Precisely as I said." The death-mage was standing above Iowenna's sarcophagus again, gazing inside. "I have conscripted you into the service of the most noble, beautiful creature who ever lived, and permitted you to wield her blessed weapon."

"Her cursed weapon! Look at this!" Blood dripped onto the floor. He yanked his dress shirt from the pack, scattering other supplies. Bunching the sleeve up for a bandage, he pressed it into place and unlatched the belt from around his leather doublet.

Zalaczar's raspy voice lilted like he was daydreaming. "Cretin. I explained it very clearly. The curse is my own creation, as is the new enchantment upon the blade to keep you alive."

None of it made sense. There was just the single goal: keep alive to keep fighting. The belt went around the makeshift bandage and he cinched it tight. The crude dressing scrubbed more diabolic acid into his skin. Swift as he could manage, Ronak took up the sword and clambered to his feet, keeping weight off the injury. "I'll break your curse right now, old man."

Reluctantly turning away from the marble box, Zalaczar beckoned. The wraith swept between them on a gust that smelled of pig iron and twisted soul. "I prefer to trust my own good judgment, so I will presume you are not so very stupid as to continue threatening me in my own domain." The necromancer walked straight through the dark mist of the wraith's form, dispersing the evil cloud for a moment. Stopping a few steps away, he continued. "Let me enlighten you further though. I am not a thick-headed, short-sighted half-orc, so foolish as to condition a curse upon my own survival. The wound ensures your subservience to my beloved. The sword ensures your survival, drawing life from your opponents to sustain your own pitiful flesh. Of course, every curse has a weak link. That, I would argue, is where the artistry actually lies. This curse can be dismantled, by using the sword to slay your love. Poetic, don't you think?"

The overflowing certainty in the necromancer's words drained Ronak of everything except despair. The room tilted. He limped aggressively to keep on his feet. Each light hop on the wounded leg made pain flare up to engulf him. Shaking his head in denial only increased the dizziness.

Zalaczar waved the wraith into nothingness. "I see this initial blood-letting has weakened you to the point that you need immediate assistance. It is fortunate you brought a victim with you to fortify you during the transition."

This was impossible. Life couldn't be overthrown with such little fanfare. To be transformed so easily into a mock-vampire? Incomprehensible. But that bizarre riddle crumpled beneath Zalaczar's hideous suggestion. Refusing with another head shake made the room tip again. Mostly to hear himself say the words, he insisted, "No. I would never do that to Aly."

"You mean, in your former life you would never have done such a thing. But today you have been re-born, little orc. You are now a servant of Lady Arkenholt. Your frivolous allegiances of the past are nothing." He considered Ronak for a moment. "Yet I will make this first step simpler."

Ronak went on guard. As best he could.

Zalaczar walked away, going toward Alyonnsa. Her horrified mewing grew louder.

Ronak hobbled forward to cut the necromancer down.

Zalaczar swirled a hand, chanted an arcane phrase, and flicked a channel of roaring wind across the chamber.

Thrown to the floor and carried tumbling across it, Ronak barely managed to keep hold of the sword amid the gale. Howling winds pinned him up against the side wall, striving to steal his breath.

When the magic storm died, Zalaczar was lifting his hand from Alyonnsa's chest.

"Get away!" Ronak wheezed.

Aly slumped to the floor, released from the paralysis. She burst into thick, scabrous coughing that wracked her tiny frame. The necromancer returned to the sarcophagus. "Your pet's lungs are filled with swamp sludge. Neither of you have the power to heal her, so she will perish in a matter of hours. Your choice is simple: kill her to sustain your life or die alongside her." He took the scabbard from the corner of the marble coffin and tossed it at Ronak's feet.

Grim rejection for the mere sake of rejecting was all that remained. "No," Ronak spat, struggling again to his feet. "I will make my own way. I'll carry her out, then someday I'll return and —"

A deafening crash shook the room. Zalaczar had pushed the sarcophagus lid completely aside, sending it crashing down to shatter on the floor. "Begone, slave. And serve your Lady well." Then he leaned forward into the open coffin.

Too exhausted for revulsion, Ronak sheathed the sword and stumbled to Aly's side.

At mausoleum's entrance, Ronak tripped and collapsed onto the starlit lawn. He twisted to his side trying to not crush Aly or snap her sun-staff. Then he lay still, breathing in the fresh air and fragrant grass.

Her rattling breath and hacking cough were growing weaker.

The journey was too long. And he had wasted time, stopping to fix the clumsy bandage. Setting her body down had been a delicious relief, until he'd realized the stone shelf was meant to hold a corpse. So he had quickly cinched the dressing tight, lifted his friend again, and limped onward through the chambers and hallways. Each step on his left foot had burned his body, mind, and heart. Each scalding jolt was laced with the necromancer's words: they didn't both have to die.

By the Blade, he was a sorry sack of refuse if he couldn't even banish the idea. And now, escaped from the tombs, it only became more clear. They weren't even halfway and he was struggling for breath almost as much as she was. He couldn't do it.

She just lay there.

It was disgustingly easy to consider saving himself. Mirreton was miles away. Saving her was impossible. But releasing her was unthinkable. What kind of friend was he? Aly had mended his body more times than he could count. She was like family, like a sister to him. Now she was drowning in contagion and there was nothing he could do.

Except end the torment.

Surprised at the cool touch of metal and leather on his hand, Ronak looked to see he was already holding the grip of his new sword. It wasn't an emblem of fortune and renown. The blade merely meant relief. For them both. He had failed Aly, leading her into a cunning death-trap. The least he could do was end her suffering.

Raising up on one elbow, he looked down on his suffering friend. She was on her side, curled up, trembling and wheezing. He had to see her differently now. Forcing his feelings down, he looked with the analytic perspective to measure an opponent, identifying weak spots and pressure points where a sliver of steel would produce the quickest death. This was the final spring of the trap and, Wayfather curse him, he was the killing blade.

Starlight glimmered on one of the brooches holding Aly's white cloak, highlighting the shape of the crescent moon.

The same shape had greeted him so many years ago when he would retreat into the attic of Grandfather's home. Staring out over the rooftops of King's Landing, relieved and a little surprised that he had survived another day, the crescent moon was often there too. That sliver of light above the dark houses and rough streets gradually unveiled a secret to a half-orc boy too small to survive in his own tribe, almost too small to survive in the city. There was something above the bullies and the abuse and the drudgery. It wasn't always visible, but if he kept climbing to the attic window each evening, sooner or later the crescent moon would return and form delicate arrangements with the first stars glowing in the twilight.

Ronak stared at the brooch. Aly was too good for this ending. So was he. It might not be much, but he could deny the necromancer's will a little longer. He knew what the moon actually was, of course, but he also knew what it meant. So he would deny the death-mage for as long as the crescent moon held the promise of escaping from the darkness.

A deep breath was all he had to prepare for the pain, but he tried to speak gently. "Let's get you home, kid."

Something moved in the night.

He glanced over and the graveyard careened while a tinny, ringing sound filled his ears. But he caught a glimpse of something prowling. Digging fingers into the grass and soil, he fought for balance amid the spinning shapes of tombstones. When the world steadied again, he surveyed more carefully.

It loped behind the low grave stones. Footsteps circled around them.

Another lucky glimpse proved the suspicion — a wolf working its way closer. But there was no way in Patch's horde that Aly was becoming a meal for some mangy scavenger tonight.

He rolled onto his back. Slow and quiet, he unsheathed Arkenholt's sword. With the other hand, he slipped his fingers under the bandage. Grinding his teeth, he dabbed some of the warm blood. Turning back onto his stomach, he coated the steel with it, then extended the sword and brushed it across the grass out in front of him.

A few moments later, the wolf stopped circling. It padded towards him, licking its fangs, snarling.

Feral growls like that demanded a reply, but Ronak caught himself. Bait didn't fight back. Instead he tried to cower from the hunter.

The wolf came forward, but not enough. It stood watching, waiting. Then Aly gave a feeble moan. The pitiful sound goaded the beast. It dashed and lunged for the kill.

The blade angled up just enough to catch this hope.

It took the wolf at the base of its throat, sliding effortlessly through its torso until the animal crashed down on him with a yelp. The beast struggled weakly for a moment, then collapsed, panting its last hot breath on Ronak's face.

Two surprises burst open.

A tidal wave of vigor swept up Ronak's sword-arm, spilled into his chest, and flooded through his body. The night poured in with it, crowding more stars into the burgeoning sky, more blades of grass into the yard, more strands of fur on the pelt. A deluge of odors flooded him. Wild fur touched with forest winds and graveyard weeds, tainted with death-panic; blood fresh and blood stale; sycamore, wild currants,   dandelion, all swamped in clover; weather-stained stone and puddles of tepid water from recent rains. From nearby, a stench of rot made him shake his head and sneeze.

Before he could trace that smell, the second invasion descended — a woman's bone-scraping shriek, drenched in defiance and rage, tore through him.

Exploding into motion, Ronak came on guard ten feet away from the wolf carcass. The tall sepulcher and surrounding gravestones stood inert, while the night breeze tugged at the bit-weed and tetterwort. The banshee had vanished.

What have you done to me! Her brutal accusation pierced Ronak's skull like an arc of lightning.

He spun and slashed. Desperation ruined the cut, but a magic blade should still bite deep. "Come out and face me!"

Would that I could, blood-spawn! The voice dropped to a callous whisper. *I'd drive a stake through each of your limbs, both your eyes, and then your heart.*

Cruel words spoken so softly launched Ronak into another terror-stricken attack. But the air was empty — a feint. He whirled back to counter the attack following the distraction. "Godsword! Where are you?"

Right in front of you, vermin.

Taking slower, deeper breaths, he raised the sword hilt. The blade's balance was delightful in its own right. The quillons and guards were as elegant as ever and the Elven script hadn't changed. Nothing new to be seen. "The priest didn't say anything about you talking."

Then he apparently didn't know very much. But since you sought information from him, you forsaken parasite, you must be even more ignorant.

The surprise transmuted into mild annoyance. At least there wasn't another battle to delay caring for Aly. "I don't have time for this." New-found vigor from the wolf made each movement crisp as he cleaned and sheathed the sword. Then he went to Aly's side.

The voice was muted, but impossible to ignore. *Listen, vampire…. By the Blade! You stinking, green-skinned, blood-sucking bastard! What did you do to her?*

"I didn't do anything," he lied. Guilt would cost time they couldn't afford right now. He scooped the halfling into his arms again. The stench of her magical infection plagued him with each weak breath she let out. But that wasn't going to stop him. He grabbed her staff and set out. Each pace jarred the left side of his body with a streak of hurt, but once he growled his way through those first bursts of punishment, he worked up to a slow jog.

At the cast iron gates marking the entrance to the graveyard, the sword murmured, *Oh Holy Wayfather…. You! Where are we? No — tell me what's wrong with her!*

Between breaths of nauseating air and flashes of cursed pain, he managed a reply. "Not to be rude …but this isn't … as easy as it looks…. So if you wouldn't … distract me…."

This is important! What happened to her?

Hoping some answers would earn a little peace and quiet, Ronak slowed to a walk. "She was poisoned."

By whom?

He rolled his eyes. "You're not actually a half-elf priest, are you?"

What? No, I'm a…or I was…. It doesn't matter! Who poisoned the halfling?

"An insane necromancer, who has sealed his fate —"

By the blade — his name! Tell me his name!

"All right! It's Zalaczar."

The voice sank to a mournful whisper. Godsword, no. Not again….

Curious now, Ronak walked a few moments more. Either the sword would explain something or demand more answers. But as the quiet seconds passed, it felt more like she was grieving. Good company. He braced himself, then started once more on his penance.

To be Continued….

Check out more cartoons like this....
www.leftycartoons.com

POETRY

"Genuine poetry can communicate
before it is understood."

–T.S. Eliot

Wordless

The poem was but - a wisp
Of a thought.
Jumbled up in a box
Inside his head,
Under the staircase
Of an enigmatic place,
Where no light shone — ever.
Weeping windows of a
Wintered soul,
Beyond the door a path
To the poet's poetry.

~ Robin McNamara

Grey

A cloudling am I.
Many a droplet I carry.
Together we fly,
miles along the boundless sky.

Dirty land awaits me below.
Along the shores, I would flow
if ever I happen to fall below.
Should I? or should I not?

Something holds me back.
Is that the fear of getting dirty?
Or is that the reluctance to leave my sky?
I wish I had an answer!

With time, grew my thoughts,
into a mammoth rock in the sky,
black and bulky, strange and sulky.
Not a choice left with me,
I poured down to those barren lands.

A tender touch was all they needed,
to reinstill life in those arid lands,
which would have happened a lot earlier,
but for my grey indecisiveness.

~ Rahul Palulli

Gemini

The wind that carries it all
the good, the bad, the things that matter
the things that don't.
The breath that eases afflictions
and halts the suffocating feeling in my lungs.
The moments that felt heavy,
and those inescapable burdens I was too tired to carry.
They fly and they dissipate.
They contort and they disintegrate
into nothing at all.
The freedom that is the wind,
and the lightness that it possesses,
It is you, and you are to me,
the energy that transgresses.

~ Ana Lico

The Last Poet

Eyes blind,
ears deaf,
tongue mute,
fingers finally still.

The last poet has died.

No one has cried,
nor are any aware yet,
the last poem has been written.

No more will flow,
words.

Words of
Anger,
Beauty,
Enlightenment.

Words of
Discontent,
Joy,
Enhancement.

Words of
Hate,
Love,
Enchantment.

No more words will flow.
No eulogy left to give.

For the last poet has died.

~ Joanna Ballard

Will Write For Chocolate

Twitter: @inkyelbows

WillWriteForChocolate.com   by Debbie Ridpath Ohi

Check out more cartoons like this....

www.inkygirl.com

Silent Descent

Languid lusty laze-a-bout.
Hands high on the back of your neck.
Transitory loss of self,
gasping in the heat.
This chanced moment comes
as falling stars glance the moon
and drop to earth
with a silent descent.
Wishing. Waiting. Wanting more.
Panting. Pushing. Praying, please.
Knowing that the end comes too soon
and the beginning starts too late.
Never did i think it could
as i always wished it would.
It came to me and came to me
as i dropped to earth in my silent descent.

~ Heather Bansemer

What is a Dream?

What is a dream?
Could it be as it had always seemed?

Is a dream a series if climatic events?
Is it a makeup of all the life you've spent?

Are dreams something we just think happens?
That since we're sleep what we thought happens never
happened?

In dreams does it go as we say?
Or is it just our mind at play?

Is a dream where all images go astray?
Is a dream what we live every day?

May a dream just be a normal sleep pattern?
That it isn't special trips to Saturn

Maybe a dream isn't the colors in every hue
I have found that a dream is a reflection of your inner you

~ Natrissa Baxter

Pass Us By

I thought that it was a "circle of life",
I thought it was something to be treasured,
I thought it was a gift so precious,
But it isn't so much to it, what is it really?

Holding hand in hand,
We can't seem to agree,
I wish nothing more than to be happy,
I want to be happy with you,

It's too short, and it's full of emotion,
It's confusing,
It's a make shift of everything possible,
But even so, it can't pass us by,

Not today, not tomorrow,
However, the way we are going,
There will be no tomorrow for either of us,
And in turn, life will pass us by.

~ Tony Devent

Genesis

Mothers love held him in
As long as strength allowed
Till in pain and cries
She gave him up to the sun
That would seek to scorch him
To brighten then to burn

Pure contrast in his eyes
He sees faces, all smiles
Things to know will come in time

But his tears roll swiftly
As fear grips his heart
Where will he find the warmth
Which was his surround
In the purest home which mother built

His cries of want go out
As tiny limbs travail

Slowly his cries submerge
He can feel it again
The care
The familiarity of home

Till he learns to smile
He can only stare
As mothers tears
From loving eyes
Answer his despairing cries

He must belong here
In the arms of love.

~ Derwin Emmanuel

Fireworks

Its slow way across the sky
breaks and bursts
like god unzipping
a hole in the night.

But for all its slow
and stately unraveling,
it's done
and done
oh so fast
and god just laughs
at these fools
who would squander fire.

~ Jacob Evans

Seduction

It sits in the center of a china plate
surrounded by a dainty design of pink roses.
The creamy, pastel yellow mixture
delicately balanced on a golden crust
tempts me beyond resistance.
With anticipation I push my fork
through the sensuously smooth filling.
Slowly, I put the luxurious creation in my mouth,
closing my lips gently
to feel the silky texture between them
as I pull the fork from my mouth.
The texture is divine.
The pleasure is intense.
I desire more.
I anxiously anticipate the next moment of pleasure.
It seems I simply can't resist the seduction
of a delicious piece of cheesecake.

~ Veronica Free

Nemo Seduces the Sea

Under a summer's half-moonlight,
Seeing the rebirth of the stars above,
Next to the Black Castle I wrote,
And sung a melody from a song,
Smiling to the shining sea,
Kissing my feet with its flood,
Opening my eyes to the lore,
Unlocking my heart with the keys of love,
And then, I wrote a poem…
A poem on wings turned to dust.
The fence of the castle my eyes beholds,
The wind from the south blows,
Stone people kissing in the north,
Nemo writing nonsensical poetry,
An Indian playing a flute in a song…
The blistering sea its waters flows,
A tale of infinite dreams I prayed to God,
An unfair & incoherent love story,
A dramatic & peaceful love:
Nemo loved the sea below.
In love with these dark waters,
A magic island floating far across,

Keeping imprisoned Nemo's truest love,
An angel whose wings he lost…
Each night of half-moon,
Nemo seduces the sea with words of love,
To find the tears of rage,
And to free his feelings & woe,
To find his fallen angel,
To write him letters of sweet words...

~ Hector J. Fuentes

Revel

Jazz trumpet
through a window
during mid-day sun

notes
over and over again
each time new

never losing
the basic feel of sadness
mixed with anger

sounds of
hail and fire
mixed with blood
hiss of fire
cast into the sea
silence
of a shooting star
twilight coming
to question mankind
bottomless pit
of a heroin haze
desperate notions
of a final revenge

pale angel
in black cotton;
quiet, she trembles,
a small book
open in her hands

sits
on the low curb
of a rundown street
on the edge of a city
at the end of time

listens
to the trumpet
as thousands of stars
slowly push the sun
below the horizon

she has
a new face, untouched
by the aging trumpet's
earthly anguish;
eager to appease

at her feet,
in the winds' swirls
of the street's trash
and broken glass,
is her small purse

the purse holds
seven golden vials filled
with the wrath of her god
who considers us all
to be his own children

Grace be unto us all, and peace . . .

Jazz trumpet
through a window
during midnight's cool,
the basic feel of sadness
mixed with anger

silence
of a shooting star

Grace be unto us all, and peace . . .

pale angel
in black cotton;
quiet, she trembles,
on the low curb
at the end of time

Grace be unto us all, and peace . . .

~ Tom Geddie

Forty Years After Dawn

We burnt drums and exiled the drummers
Still holding cows for other villagers to milk
Undergarments of the banks stink like garbage
Forty years after dawn
State plans still dressed in torn overalls of the parliament
Bullet speak louder than ballot
Forty years after dawn we discovered no totem of truth
And flowers of freedom never bloom
Forty years after dawn
Blood smells more toxic than pesticides in the lungs of the
cities and nostrils of the villages

~ Mbizo Chirasha

Check out more of these comics at…
www.dieselsweeties.com

HAIKU
Themes

April 2019 Theme

"Spring"

Spring is beginning.
Awake to that which is new
and feels familiar.

~ Marcus Blake

Dear blooming Malus
You are the remembrance tree
Spring snowy blossoms

~ Anonynmous

Spring bird-song babble
Waiting by the greenhouse shade
Chestnut tree shelter

~ Anonynmous

BARMAID, CAN YOU SAY WITH *100% CERTAINTY* THAT GOD DOES NOT EXIST?
NO, I CAN'T

THE LACK OF *GOOD* EVIDENCE FOR YOUR GOD MAKES THE PROBABILITY OF ITS EXISTENCE *VANISHINGLY SMALL*, BUT *NOT* ZERO
SO YOU ADMIT THAT THERE'S A POSSIBILITY?
YES

THEN WE WIN!
BECAUSE *WE* CAN SAY WITH 100% CERTAINTY THAT GOD *DOES* EXIST!
BUT *HOW* CAN YOU SAY THAT WITH 100% CERTAINTY?

BECAUSE WE'RE 100% CERTAIN!
CHECK. MATE.

Articles *and* Editorials

New Beginnings

By Veronica Free

Have you ever felt like you would just like to start over? Maybe things aren't going well for you at the moment. Or possibly, you feel you aren't moving forward in life. You can most definitely start over. You can experience a new beginning and move forward.

Traditionally, the first day of January is celebrated as a day of new beginnings. However, there are various other dates and occasions that offer us a chance for a new beginning. It can be to our advantage to make positive use of each opportunity.

Birthdays offer an excellent opportunity to begin again. On your next birthday, take time to review the year gone by. Set new goals for the upcoming year. Write goals down and check your progress throughout the year. Look around your home and work space. Do you have clutter there that is hindering your tranquility or productivity? If so, begin clearing the clutter immediately and continue until you live and work in an organized, uncluttered place. Do you have emotional baggage weighing you down on your special day? This would be a good time to resolve the issues from your past that are troubling you. If there is no possible resolution to the issue, then release it. Grant yourself emotional freedom. Open up space for positive thoughts. On your birthday, give yourself the gift of a new beginning.

An anniversary date can be a good opportunity for a new beginning. Are you celebrating the anniversary of a relationship that needs rejuvenating? If so, find a way to spice up the relationship. If you have reached the anniversary date of a relationship that is hindering you from following your own heart's desire, access the situation and find a way to begin following your heart and fulfilling the dreams you have. If you are celebrating the anniversary date of a job change or promotion, check to see if you are still moving forward in this area of your life. Set higher goals if you have been treading in the same position for too long. Use any anniversary date as a time to begin moving forward and reaching higher.

One of the best occasions for celebrating a new beginning is the change of seasons. Use the summer and winter solstice as a time to reflect on the past month, access your present situation, and make plans for the upcoming months. Correlate your goals with the season. Allow nature to assist you in your progress. Each new season offers opportunities for change and growth. Take advantage of these opportunities. Change is necessary in order for progress to occur. Change is good. Nature reminds us of that fact at least four times each year.

New Year's Day, birthdays, anniversaries, and the change of seasons all.

SHOOT THE CRITIC AND REMAKE THEM

The Right Way to Critique Film and TV

By Marcus Blake

How often do we feel that Movie and TV critics get it wrong? How many times have we complained about a website like Rotten Tomatoes getting it wrong when it comes to rating movies or TV shows? I know I have and I'm a critic. And, I also know that it's always a matter of an opinion, there is no empirical proof that one review is the absolute truth or should be taken as gospel. It's also easy to say that those who can't create become critics and while that may not necessarily be true, the one thing that is true is that most people are critics in their own way and love to make stupid comments on the internet furthering the notion that critics are just hacks. I can go on and on about that, but I think the only thing that matters is the opinion of the audience. If you like something and the critics don't, who cares, as long as you enjoyed it and get your money's worth..that's all that really matters. Now, don't misunderstand me, this article is not about tearing down a profession which I happen to be a part of, but about re-examining how we critique things and asking the right questions when it comes to our critiques.

Too many times I feel like the other critics just get it wrong and not that my opinion is more holy than theirs, but what I criticize more than anything when it comes to critics is their perspective, not their opinion. It seems like they have a narrow viewpoint when it comes to their critiques. What it boils down to are the questions that we ask. Yes, there are certain criteria for every good review such as grading the performances by the actors, how well the movie or tv show flowed from an editing standpoint, how good it looked, and most importantly, how will the story connect to the audience. Yes, all of these things should be taken into consideration when reviewing a Movie or TV show. But I think there are only three questions that we really need to ask ourselves when it comes to judging whether something is bad, merely entertaining, or truly great. And that's what this article is about, critics finally asking the right questions, especially for websites like Rotten Tomatoes, which sways an audience as if they have a messiah complex and their website is like the Bible for reviews. And I'll dispense with that myth right now, it shouldn't because they don't ask the right questions. When the right questions are not asked, Movies and TV shows get judged too harshly. The other problem is using the exact same criteria to critique a Movie or TV show every genre. Marvel superhero movies shouldn't be critiqued in the same way as *Schindler's List*. But like I said, it's about asking the right questions.

There are three basic questions we should ask when critiquing a Movie or TV show... only three and yes, it's that simple. The first question is did the Movie or TV show inspire me or elicit such an emotional response that I felt something powerful from watching it. The second question is was the movie or show so bad that it couldn't keep my attention or I couldn't find anything that I liked about it. The third question is did the movie entertain me even if I never watch it again.   These three questions or a variation of these questions essentially gives us three different categories that we can put Movies or TV shows in. That's right, only three categories. But I will also admit that there are subcategories to those three main categories and that's for a whole different debate.

Basically Movies and TV shows can put into three categories ... It's either great, bad, or entertaining. Most of what we watch is just entertaining. It's mindless and it won't change the world, but it will entertain us and make us forget about our troubles at least for a little while. It's escapism. A good example is pretty much any Charlie Chaplin and Buster Keaton film. We regard their films as classics to the point that everybody should watch them. I agree with that, but they're not inspiring. They're not going to change the world in any way. They are pure escapism, giving the audience a good laugh. And everybody needs a good laugh. But I put all of these films in the entertainment category and there's nothing wrong with just entertainment unless you try to put a political agenda in the movie. Can't Wonder Woman just be an entertaining Superhero film without some feminist agenda? I mean, we already now she's a bad ass and can be entertained by that without the film blatantly telling the audience that.

We like different movies and TV shows for different reasons and that's why we can't judge them for the same reasons. Once critics understand that or even an audience then it makes it easier to accept what a movie or TV show really is and judge it fairly. There's a lot of shows or films I know aren't great, but it's entertaining enough that I would watch it again. To get right down to it, let's talk about what are truly great movies... the movies that inspire and fill us with emotion that our lives can be changed. These movies are *Schindler's List* or *12 years a Slave* or even *Room*. These films are the perfect example of I'm listening an emotional reaction to the point where we can't ignore the subject matter and makes us view the world in a better way. These kinds of films help us find our humanity. *Philadelphia* was the first movie that I truly recognized as a great film based on what I described above and it changed my worldview because growing up in a Christian conservative household where homosexuality wasn't that accepting as a lifestyle, that film made me realize they were people we could die of horrible diseases and still be discriminated against. That's he perfect example of a great movie. And even though we may never watch these movies over and over, we recognize why they're great and even why they may deserve awards. *Band of Brothers* is a great TV show for the very reasons. However, most films that we see aren't going to fit in the "great" category. They aren't even going to stand the test of time. I see hundreds of films every year from mainstream movies to independent film and if I'm lucky, maybe 1% are in the great category. The ones that can make me cry... Those are the ones I know are great and even though my list may not be as long as some, I have a pretty good list of the films or TV shows that can do that.

Since most movies and TV shows fit in the entertainment category, let's really look at what kind of films or TV shows these are. Pretty much any comedy, action, superhero movie or TV show will go here. Some science-fiction movies or TV shows can will make the great category because of the allegories they tell. Gene Roddenberry, the Creator of *Star Trek* one said, "science fiction is a way of thinking, a way of logic that bypasses a lot of nonsense it allows people to look directly at important subjects." I agree and that's why I think movies like *Equilibrium* would go in the "great" category or even the reboot of *Battlestar Galactica*. *Game of Thrones* definitely belongs there because it's basically Shakespearean stories. However, I think we can all agree that pretty much any 80s action movie or rom-com pretty much goes in the "entertainment" category. I love *Die Hard* and yes, it is a Christmas movie, there's nothing special about it except the fact that it's pure entertainment just like *Christmas*

Vacation. And as much as I love superhero movies I can't put them in the same category as *Schindler's list* or *12 years a Slave*. Sure, they may be a modern form of mythology, but it's not original storytelling and they aren't going to change the world. That also goes for Christopher Nolan's Batman trilogy, which is generally regarded as the best superhero or comic book set of movies. It's entertainment and as long as we are entertained by them, then to judge them as bad forms of entertainment is misleading. We are in the Golden age of superhero movies and TV shows. They aren't going to change our lives or inspire us to do great things. They may not be great compared to something like *Citizen Kane*, but if we can watch it again, then should they be judged harshly. I can complain about Michael Bay as a filmmaker all day long, but I don't even judge his movies too harshly because I know what I'm getting... lots of action and nothing of substance, unless you consider explosions substance in movies.

I've had this ongoing debate for the last couple of years about the *Justice League* movie with Ben Affleck, Henry Cavill and Gal Gadot, that it wasn't really that bad of a movie. And I know a lot of people still criticized it because *Batman versus Superman* wasn't really that good and its easy to compare *Justice League* to it as being that good either. But they're superhero movies, all they're meant to do is entertain. Nerds can be the harshest critics, especially if a superhero movie doesn't adhere to the actual comics. I know, I've complained about that in the past, but then I realized. If you wanted to be purely like the comics, then read the comics and look at the movies for what they are... They're just copies of the story while using the comics as source material. All we can hope for is to be entertained. Hopefully we're entertained enough that will watch the movie again and I've watched the *Justice League* movie a dozen times and still enjoy it for what it is. It doesn't replace my love for the actual comic books. I know what kind of a movie it is. It was fun and that's all it's meant to be so when critics and audiences criticized it as being a shity movie, especially on rotten tomatoes, I'm left to wonder... were you expecting this movie to be *Schindler's List* and win an academy award? Did you expect it to be *The Avengers* movie, which is simply just a fun and entertaining action movie…nothing more. But this gets to the Crux of my problem with professional critics. Either you're just being critical for the sake of being critical because it'll create controversy on the Internet and get you a few more readers. Or you're judging every movie or TV show the same way which is a disservice to your profession. I'm not saying that every critic is this way. Even some of the ones that I disagree with are not this way and I respect what they do because I know they are objective.

In 2018 when *Bohemian Rhapsody* came out, the Queen biopic told through the perspective of Freddie Mercury's bandmates, it received some very serious criticism for not being completely true. Well, any kind of dramatic biopic is never completely true. This is another example of criticisms being misleading. Bohemian Rhapsody was not meant to change the world and no matter how inspirational you think Queen's music might be, this is simply a movie where the music is its own character. Meaning, you're meant have fun with his movie and enjoy the music, which any fan of Queen will. I didn't look at Bohemian Rhapsody as a great movie the same way I do with films like Schindler's List. It's entertaining with a magnificent performance by Rami Malik as Freddie Mercury, plus music you just can't help but sing to. The only way to truly judge this film is by how fun it is to watch especially as a Queen fan. If it doesn't entertain you that's one thing, but if you're criticizing the movie because it's not accurate enough or the perspective is one-sided then you misjudge the movie for what it is and you really just wanting a documentary about Queen. *Bohemian Rhapsody*, it's just a dramatization with great music. My grandmother was always fond of saying that if you didn't have anything nice to say that don't say it at all. It's a nice sentiment and I think you can apply the same philosophy when being a critic, but instead of not saying anything because it's not nice... I suggest don't judge a film or show unless you actually know what kind of film or show your critiquing.

I completely understand if a movie is intended to be inspirational and change our worldview, but falls completely short. Yes, those movies should be criticized for being bad. I recognize the fact that Green Book which won the academy award in 2019 for best picture is a good movie and the performances are fantastic, especially that of Viggo Mortensen, However, I also don't think it's one of the most inspirational films of all time because it whitewashed a lot of things about its characters and what really happened even to the point that the family of the main subject of the film complained. And let's not forget that you pretty much just made another *Driving Miss Daisy* movie, which that movie was an incredible film marked by the great performances Morgan Freeman and Jessica Tandy. I personally believe that to truly be a great film it must be unique and something we've never seen before. *Blackkklansman* which I personally believe should have won the academy award for Best picture is a unique film that deals with the subject of racism and that when it comes to respect in the workplace the color of your skin doesn't matter... I do put that into the category of great movies. But this leads us into the category of what makes a bad film.

Yes, there are truly bad films that have no redeeming value. I'm not talking about films that are bad, but we have an appreciation for like B Rated horror movies. Everything that Mystery Science Theater 3000 makes fun of I think is a bad movie, but something that we can have an appreciation for... Those movies that are so bad they're good! We all have films like that. And I'll give you a good example. I had a girlfriend make me watch *How to Lose a Guy in 10 days* with Matthew McConaughey and Kate Hudson.... It really is kind of a terrible movie, but it's funny and it fits within that category that it's so bad it's good and that's why you watch it again. If we made a list of those type of movies it would be very long. But some movies come along that are just so bad from the performances to the cheap CGI that ruins how the film looks, right down to how it was that it was edited. One the worst movies I've ever seen was Nicolas Cage in *Left Behind*. It was a remake of the biblical themed movies starring Kirk Cameron and I can't believe

I'm actually going to say this but the Kirk Cameron version was actually better. That's not saying much because they're both terrible. But Nicolas Cage's version of the movie had bad acting, the editing was absolutely terrible, and the effects look like they came from a twelve-year-old student who is making his first film for a school project. The biblical themes aren't even the worst part of this movie and there are a lot of biblical theme movies that are just horrible. But then again, there are a lot of biblical theme movies that are good like *Miracles from Heaven* with Greg Kinnear. Another example of a really terrible movie is *The Room* from Tommy Wiseau.... Generally regarded as the worst movie ever made despite its cult status as the type of movie that is so bad it's good. Honestly, it's just a bad movie, despite some fans who view it as some kind of satirical masterpiece or a film that makes fun of itself. It's true that some films are bad because they're trying to do too much or don't have enough of a budget to do what they really wanted. But there are a lot of great movies that were filmed on low budgets and somehow cobbled together a great story through good editing and good performances. I've seen a lot of independent films that fit that description proving that you don't need a huge budget to make a good film. Also, I don't think every art film is necessarily bad as long as you know what it is. A lot of them get labeled as bad films because they are artistic and maybe you have to think too much when watching them, but I don't think of them that way as long as you are discussing the film. If you walk out of the theater and you're talking about it, then there must be something redeeming about that film.

Vanilla Sky may not have been a great film overall compared to all the films we mentioned in our "great" category, but there is something redeeming about it because we pretty much all walked out of the theater discussing what we just saw and the meaning within the film, which I suppose is what Cameron Crowe, the director's intention truly was. Even these kind of films have their value. But I'm not opposed to bad movies or TV shows especially the ones that tread the line of just entertainment to being a bad show. After all some of them should be made for *Mystery Science Theater 3000*. Riffing on movies is a great pastime.

I think it's time for critics to finally examined movies for what they are and that's why I believe there's only three categories. And within those categories are just three questions that we ask whether the movie or TV show is worth seeing. Just because something is merely entertaining doesn't mean it's absolutely horrible or that we won't watch it again. Most of what we see isn't meant to inspire or change the world. Entertainment is escapism and that's the point. Sure, there's a whole other category of arts films that are meant to be discussed.... they certainly have their own place when it comes to filmmaking. Terrence Malick films are the perfect example. Sometimes they fit within the category of great and sometimes they may be bad, but they're worthy of discussion and should be appreciated for what they are. The same way a Transformers movie is just pure entertainment even when it's bad. *Transformers: The Last Knight* wasn't really good, but it was entertaining to a point and I didn't feel like I wasted my time especially in a movie theater day drinking. But I wouldn't judge this movie the same way I do *Schindler's List.* Perhaps instead of having one meter to judge all movies we should have three different kinds of rating systems for the truly great films or bad films or the ones that just entertain us. There's a lot of films that have more redeeming value than we give them credit for if we were just to evaluate them based on the categories that I'm suggesting.

As a hardcore Star Wars fan, I clearly admit that the Star Wars Prequels are not that good compared to the original trilogy, but I judge them on their own merit that are filled with lots of action and lovable characters and then give us a good backstory of what it was like before the empire took over the Galaxy. We get to see the rise in the birth of Darth Vader and the best lightsaber duels in the Star Wars saga and that's more important than the really horrible dialogue. But that's because they're only entertaining and aren't going to get into the great category like *The Empire Strikes Back.* And as much as I love The big Lebowski oh, it's not really that great of a film, but it's a lot of fun with a lot of great one-liners and that's why we watch it. So for us critics, it's time we start evaluating movies for what they are or what category they should go in. There's nothing wrong with saying that it may not be a very good movie, but I enjoyed it because it entertained me for a little while. That's pretty much every Tom Cruise movie, except maybe three, *The Last Samurai, Born on the 4th of July, and Rain Man.* To be honest, John Wayne who made over 200 movies in his career, including B Rated Westerns he did in the 30's before he was really famous...I would say that only five of his films are truly great and the rest are just entertaining. As a John Wayne fan, I can love them all because I know what the films are.

And if I can venture an opinion like C-3PO from Star War, whether you care for it or not, if you're the type of critic that just wants to be harsh about a movie because you think it should meet the same standards as a great movie like *Citizen Kane*, then either you don't really know storytelling or you're just being an asshole who can't appreciate good entertainment even when the film or show is not really that good. That's certainly not every critic out there, but there are definitely a few whose reviews I've read and leave me shaking my head wondering why you're in this profession. You're no better than the critics who purposely give low ratings to movies on rotten tomatoes and leave ridiculous comments because that's the only way you feel like your voice can be heard or you're under some misguided notion that you're a rebel with a cause, trying to take down the system. Only a few films and TV shows can truly be called "great" and while there are a lot of bad films and TV shows that probably never should have been made, most of what we watch is just pure entertainment and should be judged weather iT entertains us or not and that's why I still think *Justice League* is a pretty damn good movie because I'm entertained every time I watch it and it doesn't have to be a movie like *Citizen Kane* or *Schindler's List*. Besides, for human beings, there's only so many movies or TV shows that should fill us with emotion and inspire us to the point that were crying at the end. That's too emotion to take on, on a daily basis and that's why we need more entertaining films. If we judge a movie or TV show for what it really is and the majority of them aren't really that bad... they've done their job when comes to entertainment. Like I've I said, it's time to reexamine how we critique movies and TV shows and stop judging them all the same way. We start by shooting the critics that do that and remake them or maybe just reboot them. If Hollywood can reboot films, we can certainly reboot critics especially the one Rotten Tomatoes so that can finally judge a film or TV show properly.

Check out more cartoons like this....
www.leftycartoons.com

BUSINESS LOANS
AVAILABLE
APPROVAL RATE: 94.4%
CALL or TEXT
214-681-8400

A MIXED BAG *Of* FACT and FICTION

Platinum Status Americans

When You Can Commit Crimes and Get Away with It

By Bob Jensen

It's been a week of celebration at the White House. While the Mueller Report has dominated the news, there's another significant event that has not been covered as much, but is connected to the Mueller Report. President Donald Trump has been initiated into a Platinum status club reserved for only the most powerful people in the world. People that are so rich and powerful, they will never be prosecuted for their crimes, no matter the evidence against them. The club doesn't have an official name but it's been around since the 1970s. It was unofficially started by Richard Nixon, who was facing impeachment and prosecution after the Watergate Scandal. The purpose of this club is to make sure that certain people do not go to jail or can't be prosecuted no matter the crime, especially if there's mounting evidence.

It's true, this sounds like something you would find in a movie about a secret society we're in the real world this couldn't possibly happen because all things are fair and people are held accountable for their actions. It's a nice pipe dream, but that's not the way it's really works in America. And our President, Donald Trump is the perfect example. He will never be prosecuted after being initiated into this special club any more than Hillary Clinton will ever be prosecuted for breaking at least three federal laws while she was Secretary of State. Because powerful people just don't go to jail, this upsets the balance or the status quo in the United States. And keeping the status quo is more important when it comes to maintaining the fabric of American society. There has been a long tradition of powerful people who have never been prosecuted and it goes all the way back to Andrew Johnson, who was impeached, but never thrown out of office. He still got to be president. It's usually the poor that end up taking the blame or getting falsely accused of crimes. They're easy to put away because they don't have enough money to defend themselves and they're certainly not powerful enough to avoid prosecution. It also helps if you're NOT white. Again, this helps keep the status quo in American society.

The last couple of weeks Americans has been on the edge of their seat wondering what was truly in the Mueller Report, but it doesn't matter because nothing will come of it. One Department of Justice official even said, "the Mueller report could have unequivocal evidence a Donald Trump was an imposter or a Russian spy and we still wouldn't prosecute because we just don't do that to really powerful people who are rich." I honestly can believe that because I think there's been a long tradition of rich and powerful people who constantly get away with it even before America was a nation. It's a tradition that stems from English aristocracy and royalty. If you have money, are Protestant, and Anglo-Saxon, you can get away with anything. Honestly, if that wasn't true, would Donald Trump have ever been allowed to run for President.

The Mueller report may be exciting news, but at the end of the day the truth does not matter. Evidence is not important. Keeping the status quo in the United States is more important...if the rich and the powerful are held accountable for their actions and can be prosecuted that might actually demonstrate we have a truly free and democratic society. But that goes against everything America really is. Nations are built upon one or more two classes of people getting screwed over by the system because that's what maintains the peace. And that's why we have ethnic groups that are poor, which are an easy target. So the big news really shouldn't be about the Mueller Report that doesn't really matter anyway or how many people give damaging testimony about our president's criminal actions. The more important news is how another powerful person has gained his Platinum Status in American society where he will never be prosecuted for any of his crimes. This is important because it gives us all hope that one day we can be just as rich and powerful and do the same no matter how unlikely that is. It's much like people voting against their own economic interest and allowing the super-rich to have the best tax breaks because one day that may be just like them and we'll get those tax breaks despite the fact that realistically that will never happen. Then again America is not about realistic endeavors, but creating false narratives to trick citizens into voting against their own interests while the superrich and powerful rob us blind and get away with it.

Bob Jensen
Reporter & Columnist
The Squeeze
The more true news network!

...ARE YOU SURE YOU DON'T HAVE STOCK HOLMES SYNDROME?
THE HOUND OF THE BASKERVILLES
OUND OF KERVILLES
THE HOUND OF THE BASKERVILLES

500 FREE
Business Cards

Premium Cards, 14pt Card Stock,
Full Color, Front and Back,
Glossy or Matte Finish

Call Today
(888)
901-4665

www.bizproshop.com

Email us to find out how you can get 500 FREE business Cards. info@bizproshop.com or call (888) 901-4665

SUBMIT

We are always looking for submissions. We are looking for Short Stories, Poetry, Editorials and Articles (Non Fiction) and Cartoons / Comic Strips.

Submit your work to www.starvingwriters.net

Email us your submissions at...

submission@starvingwriters.net